NIKKI POWERGLOVES

VS the Power Outlaws

David Estes

D1417214

Jacket art and design by Winkipop Designs

For Katee, who encouraged her grandmother to contact me.
See? Kids really DO have superpowers!

And for all the funny, smart, amazing kids in
Mrs. Clanton's 3rd grade class of 2015.
You rock!

Adventures

1

The meanest of the mean

"You smell," Naomi said, holding her nose. She glared at Jimmy in that way of hers that made him want to pee his pants.

"It's not me—it's *him*," Jimmy said, pointing at Peter. He couldn't help but snicker, because he knew exactly what his old friend was doing: Practicing. Peter was wearing his green beret with the picture of the finger holding a nose that gave him the power to produce exceptionally smelly gas so potent it could knock his opponents right off their feet. Lately he'd been trying to hone his flatulation skills, much to the annoyance of all of the other Power Outlaws who were forced to constantly run from the room, their eyes watering and nostrils stinging.

Naomi tossed her long dark hair and turned her deadly stare on Peter Powerhats, who was sniffing the air. Every part of Peter was large, from his feet to his ears, and yes, even his nose. *The better to sniff with*, Jimmy thought. "Knock it off, you big oaf," Naomi commanded.

In response, Peter let out a massive fart that seemed to vibrate under their feet. "Get down!" Jimmy yelled, rushing out of the warehouse they'd been using as their secret hideout. The smell seemed to hit him from behind all at once, picking him up and knocking him off his feet. He landed in the dust outside, gagging and trying not to breathe in the noxious fumes.

When he looked up, half-blinded by tears and dust, he saw silver slippers attached to silver legs attached to a silver body. A metal robot stood before him, laughing a metallic laugh. "And you call yourselves 'Power Outlaws,'" Sue Powerslippers said. "More like Power Morons." She was currently Robo-Sue, one of her favorite powers to use when Peter was practicing his super farts. After all, robots didn't have a sense of smell, so his stinkiness didn't affect her.

Nearby, Naomi was spitting in the dirt. "Blech," she said, pushing to her feet and smoothing out her green skirt. "If Peter does that again, I'm kicking him out of the Power Outlaws." Her Asian complexion flashed with annoyance.

Sue morphed back into her beautiful nine-year-old self, complete with golden blond hair, emerald green eyes, and California-tanned skin. "*You're* kicking him out?" she said, her voice as sweet as cherry pie. "Who made you leader?" She took a step forward, trapping Jimmy between the two girls.

"Me," Naomi said, not backing down. "I was the leader before you and your band of misfits came along, and I'll be the leader long after you're gone. Anyway, you saw the Power Rankings after *I WON* the Great Adventure. I was number two, and I should've been number one if it wasn't for that brat Nikki Powergloves. And you were…let's see…what number were you again? Oh yeah, number five."

Jimmy was feeling hot and sweaty, so he tried to squirm out from between the two rivals. He hadn't even made the top five, so this wasn't his fight. He didn't care who was leader, as long as it wasn't him. Yeah, he was tired of losing to Nikki Powergloves as much as they were, but he was also getting a little scared of her. She was too good. He'd never beat her. But maybe he'd be able to help Naomi or Sue beat Nikki.

"Where do you think you're going?" Naomi said, grabbing his arm. Jimmy tried to twist away, but already Naomi's fingers were turning green and thickening, her nails growing longer, black tufts of hair sprouting from her skin. Soon her entire body had grown, turning her into a hideously ugly and strong ogre wearing a green skirt. She held his arm tightly. *Oh no*, Jimmy thought. "ARE YOU WITH ME OR AGAINST ME?" Naomi the Ogre bellowed at him, thick wads of spit flying from her big, pink sausage lips. When she was an ogre Naomi seemed to have trouble controlling the volume of her voice.

"Um, uh, well," Jimmy stammered, his arm starting to throb from being squeezed so hard. He resisted the urge to wipe the ogre spit off his face.

There was a metallic shriek from his other side, and he felt a pinch on his left arm. "Or are you with me?" Robo-Sue said, her voice sounding like a computer. She had her robot fingers clamped around his elbow. He hadn't even seen her change back into a machine.

"I, uh, if possible, uh, I'd like to be with *both* of you," Jimmy said, hoping it was the right answer.

The moment the ogre and the robot released him, he scrambled away, watching as the distance between them closed, until they were ogre-nose to robot-nose. "I'M THE LEADER!" Naomi bellowed.

"I'm the leader!" Robo-Sue screeched.

The ground started shaking under Jimmy's feet and he fell over, hanging on for dear life. *Is it an earthquake?* he wondered. The sunshine disappeared as an enormous shadow covered all of them. He looked up, expecting to see a big cloud, but instead finding a giant bigger than Naomi the Ogre or Robo-Sue, bigger than the warehouse or any of the surrounding buildings. People on the nearby streets began screaming in terror. Jimmy wanted to scream, too, but he couldn't seem to make any sound at all, his breaths coming out in ragged huffs of hot air.

"Stop it!" Tyrone the Greek god shouted, his voice like thunder. His dark-skinned face was the size of a storm cloud, and his huge earlobes were studded with gold earrings, the source of his power. Tyrone

Powerbling reached down with fingers the size of cars. Jimmy covered his head, thinking he was about to be squashed, but then Tyrone pinched Sue between his fingers, picking her up. The robot fought him, but he was too strong. She was stuck, wriggling like a metal worm on a hook.

Naomi chuckled from deep in her throat. "I GUESS WE KNOW WHICH SIDE TYRONE IS ON," she said.

Just then, something big and hairy scuttled past Jimmy. His eyes widened as the eight-legged tarantula scurried behind Naomi the Ogre, who didn't even see it coming. All eight legs wrapped around Naomi, holding her tight, even though she flexed her big, green muscles and tried to escape. The tarantula hissed. "Tyrone issssn't on your ssside, Naomi. He'sss not on Sssue'sss ssside either. We're all on the sssame ssside."

Jimmy immediately knew who the tarantula was. Tanya. Tanya Powershirts. He knew it was her red shirt that gave her the ability to turn into a tarantula. Around the other Power Outlaws, his twelve powers didn't seem so powerful anymore. *When did I become the weakest villain around?* he wondered to himself. Sure, he had some really cool powers, like his powerstomp and rocket boots, but he couldn't compete with Greek gods, tarantulas, and ogres! He'd just do what he was told and hope he didn't get hurt. Or he could run for it, leave the Power Outlaws forever and never look back. *Yeah!* he thought, the idea sounding better and better. He was already wearing his rocket boots, the red ones with the flames on the side. He could take off and fly away, and no one would ever be able to find him.

At that very moment, Peter Powerhats stepped from the warehouse, wearing a goofy smile and his green hat. His eyes danced from Tyrone holding Sue to Tanya holding Naomi. Then he settled his confused gaze on Jimmy. That's when Jimmy remembered that Peter had the power to find powerchests. If Jimmy flew away, he'd be forced to leave his powerchest behind, otherwise Peter would be able to find him.

Jimmy could never do that. *Right?* he asked himself. "What'd I miss?" Peter asked.

Not much, Jimmy thought. *Just a fight between the meanest of the mean.*

In the blink of an eye, Naomi shrunk back to her normal self, her dark, narrowed eyes flashing with anger.

Tanya the Tarantula released her and changed back into Tanya the girl. If Sue was as pretty as a beauty queen, Tanya Powershirts was as ugly as a troll. Her eyes were crossed and her nose bent. Her dark hair was perpetually tangled and her small teeth like crooked stones. Her dry chapped lips appeared to be frowning, but Jimmy remembered that that was how they always looked. As expected, Tanya was wearing a red shirt with a cool picture of a spider on it.

A few moments later, Sue transformed back into her normal Barbie Doll self, and Tyrone shrunk from a Greek god to the unusually tall and muscly nine-year-old boy that he was.

Naomi stepped forward and everyone seemed to tense up for a second. "I don't want to fight," Naomi said, raising her hands in the air. "Well, not you guys. I want to fight the Power Council. And if you idiots would all relax for a minute, I'll tell you my plan."

For the first time all day, everyone smiled.

Well, everyone except Jimmy, who was still thinking about how it would feel to fly away from it all. He could go home, back to his old life. Yeah, he didn't have a dad, but he had a mom, even if she barely noticed when he was around. At least he would be safe. He didn't need friends, at least not dangerous ones like the Power Outlaws.

For the first time in a long time, Jimmy wasn't sure if he wanted to be a villain anymore.

2

Heroes need villains? Whaaat?

To Nikki Nickerson, the Power City was a refuge, a sanctuary, a place where she could be herself, Nikki Powergloves. And it was a place where she could have fun with her new friends and her longtime best friend and genius sidekick, Spencer Quick.

She was walking through the tunnels of the Power City with Spence right now. The Power City was hidden under thousands of tons of rock under the gray mountain and Phantom's Peak. They'd just arrived back in the Power City after checking in with their parents in Cragglyville. Because of the way time was different in the mountain, Nikki knew they'd be able to spend at least three or four days in the Power City before their parents would start to worry again.

This particular tunnel was called the Aquarium, for obvious reasons. The two walls, ceiling and even the floor were all made of glass, huge tanks of water filled with sea plants and creatures. On the sides, bright tropical fish swam past, following by an eel with an open mouth full of dagger-like teeth. Above them, crabs scuttled along the glass, their pincers clicking together. Beneath their feet, three dark shadows floated by lazily. Sharks. Nikki was glad to be on *this* side of the glass walls.

Spencer was oblivious to the scenery, trying to explain the details of some new weapon he and the other sidekicks were inventing, but Nikki found her mind wandering. She didn't understand Spencer when he used "tech speak" anyway.

Instead, she was thinking about the way they'd left things with the Power Outlaws. How angry they'd all seemed, especially Naomi, who felt she'd been cheated somehow. Nikki Powergloves was still number one in the Power Rankings. But only just barely. She knew she couldn't let Naomi take over the top spot or bad things would happen.

She also knew that the Power Outlaws would be back, and the Power Council and their sidekicks would need to be ready.

Something Spencer was saying suddenly caught her attention. "And that's how the Alien Freeze Ray works!" he announced grandly.

Nikki felt bad that she hadn't really listened to his explanation, but now at least she understood what it was. It sounded awesome. "I think that will really help us in our next fight against the Power Outlaws," Nikki said.

Spencer beamed. "Do you really think so?"

"Definitely."

They arrived at the main meeting room in the Power City, the one with the big purple couches. The whole gang was already there, from the heroes, Samantha Powerbelts, Freddy Powersocks, Mike Powerscarves and Britney Powerearrings, to the other sidekicks, Chilly Weathers and Dexter Chan.

After everyone said hello, and Spencer managed to hug every single one of their friends, they plopped down onto the couches and Mike whipped up turkey sandwiches and bags of chips for each of them. He was wearing his green scarf with the picture of the ice cream cone, which gave him the power to create food from thin air. Because of Mike, they'd never go hungry in the Power City! After the long flight from Cragglyville, Nikki was famished, and devoured her food, barely remembering to chew.

"Hungry?" Samantha asked, grinning that mischievous smile of hers. She popped a chip in her mouth with one hand while using the other hand to twirl her blond curly hair. She was wearing a peach colored belt that Nikki knew would give her the power to grow extra arms and legs.

"Mm-hmm," Nikki said, swallowing her last bite of food and licking crumbs off her fingers, which were covered with two different types of gloves. One was her blue flying glove and the other her purple super-strength glove. They're what allowed her to fly with Spencer on her back all the way to Phantom's Peak.

After washing the food down with a big gulp of water, she turned to Britney and asked, "How's your training going?"

Britney was the newest member of the Power Council, having been rescued from the lair of the Power Trappers a few weeks earlier, just before the Great Adventure began. She'd only just started learning how to really use all of her powers, which were provided by her earrings. Right now she was wearing her white angel wing earrings. Britney offered a genuine smile. "I flew so much better today," she exclaimed. "Thanks for all the tips on how to use the wind to help me. I'm not nearly as good as you, but I'm getting better."

"No problem," Nikki said, blushing. She still wasn't used to the rest of the Power Council treating her like some kind of celebrity. She was no better than them, just because she'd been ranked number one. Any one of the other heroes could easily be in her position.

Anxious to take the attention off of her, Nikki scanned the room. It was painted with each of the members of the Power Council doing amazing things. Even the sidekicks had their pictures up, using their own skills to help save the day.

Spencer was sitting off to the side, talking excitedly with Dexter and Chilly about their new Alien Freeze Ray. Chilly was spinning a coin through her fingers, occasionally making it disappear, only to pull it from Spencer's ear. The pale-skinned, dark-haired girl called herself an amateur magician, but Nikki always thought she was more of a *professional* magician. Dexter was playing with a rubber band, pulling it tight and letting it snap back. The short-limbed nine-year-old liked using rubber bands in the booby traps he was always making.

Off to the side, Freddy and Mike were whispering, pointing at the corner. Nikki followed their gaze, finding two Weebles crouching in the shadows. The creatures, which looked like half-porcupine and half-beaver, were muttering under their breaths, their strong New York accents coming through. "They've been following us everywhere," Samantha said.

Nikki glanced at her friend, then back to the Weebles. One had fur that was as bright white as freshly fallen snow, while the other wore a coat as dark as tar. "Why?" Nikki asked.

"Who knows?" Samantha said, shrugging. "The Weebles are strange."

Spencer had stopped talking to the other sidekicks and was listening to their conversation. He got up and sat next to Nikki. "I think it means something, Chowder-Heads." He started humming, the tell-tale sign that he was deep in thought.

"Like what?" Freddy asked, running his dark hands over his plump belly. He was wearing the gold wristwatch that allowed him to control the time in the Power City.

"They look like a *yin yang*," Spencer said.

"What's that?" Britney asked, absently touching her angel wing earrings.

"Here," Spencer said, tapping something into his iPad. A moment later he placed it on the table between them. The screen displayed a picture of a *yin yang*, a circle split in half by a curving line. One side was painted black and the other white. On the white side was a black dot and on the black side a white dot.

"Oh, I've seen those before," Britney said. "I just never knew what they were called. But what does it mean?"

Spencer cleared his throat and used his adult voice. He sounded so much like one of their teachers, Mr. Darcy, that it was scary. "In Chinese philosophy, a *yin yang* is the symbol of how opposite forces, in this case black and white, are also complimentary to each other. In other words, you can't have one without the other. If you don't have dark, you can't have light, and vice versa."

"Oh," Britney said. She sounded as confused as Nikki felt. *What did opposite forces have to do with them?*

Freddy was a little bit quicker to understand. "I think I get what you're saying," he said. "You're talking about us and the Power Outlaws. Without villains there are no heroes."

"Wait," Nikki said. "Are you saying that we...*need* them?" In a perfect world, she'd never have to see any of the Power Outlaws ever again.

"I don't know," Spencer said. "Maybe. I think there's more to all this than we know. The Great Adventure. The Power Rankings. Even the Weebles seem like more of a mystery than they used to be." At that, the black and white Weebles in the corner tittered to themselves and started bouncing on their butts.

Nikki wanted to know more, and she started to ask another question, but before she could, a red alarm started flashing and a screen descended from the ceiling.

Nikki knew the alarm could only mean one thing: Power Outlaws!

3

Niagara Falls

Chaos. That was the only word Nikki could think of to describe what she was seeing on the screen. The enormous waterfall sounded like thunder, or maybe like bombs exploding. People were screaming, running along the winding walkways, chased by dozens of ducks, which were quacking like crazy. There was something else strange about all of the people: Every single one of them was crying, fat tears rolling down their cheeks. The wind was blowing so hard that their hats were flying off their heads and their hair was blowing all over the place. At the bottom of the screen it read "Niagara Falls, New York."

"Hey!" Spencer exclaimed. "I've been there. Niagara Falls is the most powerful waterfall in North America and is right between the U.S. and Canada. Splish Splash!"

"What's happening to all those people?" Freddy asked, but Nikki had just spotted something unusual.

A dark-haired girl was walking toward the camera wearing a gray skirt. But that wasn't the weird thing. She was walking *on* the water at the base of the falls, a misty spray surrounding her. She looked fifty percent angelic and a hundred percent scary.

"It's Naomi Powerskirts!" Nikki said. "The other Power Outlaws must be there too. They're doing this!"

"This is bad news," Samantha said. "We need to get to Niagara Falls right away."

At that exact moment, each of the power kids' power bracelets lit up, the jewels in the center radiating light of all different colors. Nikki's was half-white and half-blue. She was already wearing one blue glove, so all she had to do was open her powerchest and replace her purple glove with the white one with the snowflake picture on it.

The other members of the Power Council were preparing, too. Samantha fastened a bright red belt with a smile on it, and then held Dexter's hand. Together, they disappeared, teleporting to Niagara Falls using her power bracelet. Freddy slipped on a pair of pink socks with brains painted on them. *Eww*, Nikki thought. He grabbed Chilly's hand and vanished. Before Mike disappeared, Nikki saw that he had wrapped a white scarf with a steering wheel on it around his neck. Only Britney, Nikki and Spencer were left.

Britney was staring at a pair of small, gold hoops in her hands. "I don't know if I can do this," she said.

Nikki took her hand. "Yes, you can. You made it through the Great Adventure, remember?"

Britney looked up at her. "But that was just a game. This is real. People could get hurt!" Her voice was high-pitched and she looked as if she might cry. Nikki didn't know what to say.

Luckily, Spencer always knew what to say. He stepped between them. "You were *chosen* to be a superhero, Britney," he said. "That means your special. And it also means you can do this."

"Special?" Britney said, her eyes searching Spencer's face. "I—I can't be special. My—my parents didn't want me. They gave me away when I was born. I grew up in a foster home. They wouldn't do that if I was worth caring about."

Oh gosh, Nikki thought. So much had happened since they met Britney that she hadn't even thought to ask her about where she came from, about who her parents were. And now there wasn't time to talk about it because their friends were already battling the Power Outlaws.

"Spencer is right," Nikki said. "Your parents, whoever they are, were wrong. They didn't even get to know you. If they did, they'd be so proud of you. We know you, and you're amazing. C'mon, put those on. We'll go together." A smile lit up Britney's face as she fastened her small hoop earrings. They looked pretty next to her smile.

Nikki held out both hands, one for Spence and one for Britney. The moment they were all holding hands, the world spun upside down and the room seemed to melt around them. Colors swirled, danced, and blurred.

And then they were there. Niagara Falls thundered down, spraying a fine mist of water through the air. The wind was howling, as if they were stuck in the middle of a hurricane. Tourists were still running from the army of quacking ducks, bawling their eyes out. In truth, Nikki felt like crying, too. Her vision blurred as tears sprouted from her eyes. *What the heck is going on?* she wondered to herself. Spencer and Britney were crying, too.

"One of the Power Outlaws is doing this!" Spencer cried.

Tears rolling down her cheeks, Nikki spotted Mike Powerscarves in a boat, the engine roaring. He was tearing through the water. On board were Samantha and Freddy. All three were crying, but they were doing their best to keep going. Freddy was shouting orders to Samantha and Mike, and Nikki remembered that his pink socks gave him the power to read people's thoughts. He knew what Naomi was going to do before she did it.

Nikki continued to scan the chaos. Naomi was running across the water, charging for the boat. But then she stopped, a huge smile blanketing her face. The smile turned to a chuckle, and then a laugh, and then she was cracking up so hard she actually started slapping her own knees. Nikki's eyes widened as she realized Samantha was *making* Naomi laugh uncontrollably using the power of her red belt.

Nearby them on the walkway, Nikki noticed another familiar kid. Tyrone Powerbling stood on the side, looking almost as tall as a man, holding a gold walking stick. He pointed it at the water and it immediately began to bubble as something black and metallic appeared, coasting across the surface.

"Torpedo!" Nikki yelled. Mike heard her and saw the missile shooting toward their boat. He yanked the wheel hard to the right and revved the engine, racing away. Nikki was about to head toward Tyrone, but then she saw a massive crocodile skimming across the water toward them. It was wearing two different slippers, one crocodile skin and one with a fluffy white duck on it. The croc could only be Sue Powerslippers. They were fully under attack by the Power Outlaws and Nikki didn't know what to do.

Spencer grabbed her arm and she whirled around. "I've got a plan," he said, wiping away his tears. Nikki let out a deep breath, relieved to have her sidekick by her side. He put his arms around Nikki and Britney, bringing their heads close together in a huddle. "Britney, you use your mini-discs to take out Tyrone so he can't shoot any more torpedoes. Me and the other sidekicks will go after Tanya and Peter, I spotted them on a rock at the top of the waterfall. I think they're the ones making us cry and blowing the wind."

"What do I do?" Nikki asked, tasting salty tears on her lips.

"You take out Crocodile Sue before she eats someone," Spencer said, half-grinning, half-crying.

Nikki grinned back. She'd been dying to get Sue back for defeating her on the Great Wall of China during the Great Adventure. "Awesome plan, Spence! Let's go!"

They broke apart and Britney immediately began throwing miniature discs toward Tyrone. The saucers smashed against him, knocking him over. His gold stick flew out of his hands as he covered his head with his arms. He wouldn't be shooting any more torpedoes anytime soon.

Mike Powerscarves was still desperately trying to steer the boat away from the first torpedo, but it was catching up to them.

Naomi was still walking on the water, laughing hysterically.

Sue the Croc was swimming toward Nikki, her long, scaly tail swishing back and forth in the water. Nikki glanced at her white glove and knew exactly what to do. She pointed her white glove at the water and thought very cold thoughts. A burst of white shot from the tip of her finger. The moment it hit the water, ice began to form, racing along toward Crocodile Sue, spreading over the base of the waterfall. Sue stopped swimming, her croc legs frozen in place. Naomi stopped walking and laughing, encased in a block of ice. Niagara Falls stopped...well, stopped *falling*, completely frozen, like an enormous ice sculpture.

The torpedo was just ahead of the ice, still churning through the water, honing in on Mike's boat. Three of her friends were about to be blown up! Nikki concentrated, trying to move her stream of ice faster and faster, until it was right behind the missile.

Just when the torpedo hit the boat, her ice hit the torpedo. There was a flash of bright flame, the boom of an explosion, and then nothing.

Nothing.

The boat was in the air, above the water, cracked in half but frozen in place. Her friends, who were about to be launched out of the boat, were suspended in the air, stuck in blocks of ice. The explosion was caught in the ice, too, just like one of Jimmy Powerboots's bombs in a bank in Cragglyville a long time ago.

Nikki exhaled, her warm breath misting in the air that was now cold because of all the ice she had made.

She didn't feel like crying anymore. The wind wasn't whipping her hair around either. Nikki craned her neck to gaze up at the top of the waterfall, and found Spencer, Chilly and Dexter, each holding funny-looking devices. The Alien Freeze Rays! They were bright orange with long spouts that almost looked like vacuum cleaners at the end. A weird blue vapor was pouring out of them, and trapped in the gas were Tanya and Peter. Tanya had on a white shirt with a picture of a guy hanging from a telephone pole, being blown by a strong wind. Peter was wearing a clear hat. Clear like tears. The sidekicks did it!

Wait. The word popped into Nikki's head in an instant, as she realized someone was missing. One of the Power Outlaws. He used to be her arch nemesis, but had recently been overshadowed by more powerful supervillains, like Naomi and Sue.

And then he was there, hovering above the frozen water, flames pouring from one of his boots, a red one with fire painted on the side. Jimmy's other boot was blue. Nikki tried to remember what power the blue boot gave him...something to do with water, she thought.

"It's over, Jimmy," Nikki said. "All your friends have been beaten."

There was something different about Jimmy, Nikki noticed. Normally he would laugh, or smirk, or say something nasty to her. Not now. He looked so serious, like he was considering her words, like he was really listening. "I—" he said, but then stopped. "I—" He couldn't seem to get the words out.

Nikki used her flying glove to rise up, until she was at the same height as Jimmy, facing him eye to eye. She pointed her ice glove right at him. "Surrender," she said.

"Hit him, Nikki, Kapow!" Spencer shouted from the top of the waterfall.

"I—" Jimmy said again. *Why does he look so confused?* Nikki wondered. *Why isn't he attacking?* She almost felt bad for her old enemy. He looked...sad.

"Jimmy, are you okay?" she asked. She didn't know why she asked him that. Why should she care whether he was okay? He was a Power Outlaw, one of the bad guys. But still, he looked so miserable.

"I—I don't have any friends," he said.

"What?" Nikki said. She couldn't help just blurting it out. It didn't make sense. He had *lots* of friends. First there was Peter and Naomi, and then Sue, Tanya and Tyrone.

"I'm just tired of being alone," Jimmy said, his voice rising. "I'm tired of...of everything!" The sadness was gone, replaced by a look of anger, his mouth twisted and his teeth clenched together like a sprung mousetrap.

"I don't understand," Nikki said. "Please, just go. Take the Power Outlaws and get out of here. You can't keep terrorizing innocent people. This is over."

Jimmy shook his head. "No. It's not. It will never be over. It's always the same. People say they like you, that they'll help you, but then they turn on you. The only thing left for me is destroying things. That's the only time I'm happy."

Nikki knew they were in trouble. She'd never seen Jimmy look so focused. He spread his arms wide, and before Nikki could do anything he began waving them around wildly, like an orchestra conductor.

There was an ear-splitting *CRAAAAAACK!* and the ice Nikki created began breaking apart into huge chunks. The blocks of ice flew in every direction, filling the air. As Nikki ducked and dived and dodged the ice, she heard Jimmy laughing hysterically, almost as if Samantha was using her red belt on him. But no, he was just laughing all on his own as he threw chunks of ice everywhere.

Ice cracked, ice split, ice shattered into a million crystalline shards.

Nikki was hit by one chunk, then another, until she was knocked back, crashing to the ground. More ice piled on top of her, until she couldn't move.

And still Jimmy laughed. He laughed and laughed and laughed until Nikki felt like she couldn't keep her eyes open anymore. The last thing she saw before she blacked out were two sets of eyes peeking at her through the rubble. The eyes were surrounded by fur, white on one side and black on the other.

The yin yang Weebles, Nikki thought, closing her eyes.

4

Splitting up

Tanya Powershirts was so mad she thought steam might be coming out of her ears.

The other Power Outlaws were arguing... *again*. Even though they'd defeated the Power Council in Niagara Falls, they couldn't celebrate for even one second. All they did was argue. Well, except for Peter, who had turned himself into jelly and was oozing around the warehouse. Tanya kind of liked Peter, even though his head was filled with rocks rather than brains. Technically, Jimmy wasn't arguing either. Instead, he was sitting in the corner wearing his red/blue/yellow boots and working on some kind of strange device with lots of wires and blinking lights. Tyrone was just standing there opening and closing his powerchest, watching it shrink and grow, shrink and grow.

So mostly it was Sue and Naomi arguing. Wanting to be the leader. Wanting to make the decisions. Tanya was starting to regret having joined the Power Outlaws. The Power Council seemed much nicer, but she knew they would never take her because she was too ugly. At school it was the same way, only the bad kids would ever hang out with her because of the way she looked. She was used to it.

"I'll lead the charge on Italy!" Naomi shouted.

"Yeah, that worked really well at Niagara Falls!" Sue shouted back.

"Like you did much better!"

"I did!"

Yeah right!"

"I did!"

"SHUT UP!" Tanya finally yelled, unable to take it anymore. While they were fighting she'd grown into one of her scariest forms, a bog monster that was even uglier than she was in real life. She was dripping slime and oozing mud, her arms and legs like rotten trees.

Sue started laughing almost immediately. Naomi followed shortly after.

"Are you supposed to be scary?" Sue asked.

"Because you're not," Naomi continued. "You look like you slipped and fell in the mud."

Sue continued where Naomi left off. "Please, ugly, disgusting creature, don't drip slime on me."

The girls' laughter reminded Tanya of school, when the cool kids would laugh at her crooked nose, or her crossed eyes. The truth was, she wanted to cry.

But she didn't. She'd learned long ago that crying only made bullies laugh harder. So instead she said what she wanted to say, her bog monster voice sounding like a weird mix between Cookie Monster and Elmo. It almost sounded as if she'd swallowed a bunch of muddy leaves. "I'm glad you find me so hilarious," she said. "But while you were arguing about who would lead the fight in Italy, I was coming up with a better idea."

"And what is that?" Naomi asked, placing her hands firmly on her hips. Tanya almost laughed when Sue put her hands on her hips, too. No wonder they argued so much—they were too much alike, almost like twin Barbie Dolls, a blonde and a brunette, beautiful and confident

24

and everything Tanya wasn't. For one second, or maybe two, Tanya wished she could be more like them.

Then she remembered how annoying they were.

"We should split up," Tanya said. This time her voice sounded like garbage being crushed by a trash compactor.

To her surprise, they didn't laugh at her. Naomi looked at Sue, and Sue looked at Naomi.

"You know what?" Naomi said. "I think our hideous friend…"

"…came up with a brilliant idea," Sue finished.

"We'll split up," Sue and Naomi said simultaneously, as if it was their idea and not Tanya's.

I'm not your friend, Tanya thought. *I don't have any friends*. But she didn't say that. She said, "Naomi and Tyrone will go to Italy, Jimmy and Peter to the mountain, and Sue and me can take on the tomb."

"Those morons on the Power Council will never know what hit them," Naomi said, grinning.

Sue grinned back.

Tanya stomped away, leaving a trail of mud behind her.

5

Never take "no" for an answer

Axel loved being up high. His massive eagle's wings were spread out, letting him glide on the wind without having to flap them hardly at all. He made lazy circles in the sky, relishing the feeling of the sun on his face and the breeze rustling his blue windbreaker.

Being up high was way better than being down there, on the earth. The earth was full of problems, but they looked so much smaller when he was flying. The houses were small, the cars were smaller, and his problems seemed the smallest. Up here he didn't have to hear his parents talking about moving again, and they were *always* talking about moving. He also didn't have to think about how the Power Outlaws attacked Niagara Falls, how he watched the ice crumbling around the Power Council on the news, how he had turned the TV off and ignored it.

Up here, he didn't have to think about how he didn't go to help them.

And yet that was all he could think about.

"It's not my fight," he said out loud, trying to convince himself. "I'm not on either side. I'm a loner. I don't need anyone else."

He wanted it to be true, because it's how he'd always been. Every year or two his parents would move for their jobs. They were both in the military, which meant they got moved around a lot. Axel hated it. Seeing new places was kind of cool, he guessed, but he never really felt like he had a home. Not a real one. He never bothered to make friends, because he knew he'd just have to leave them eventually. He was better off being a loner. And both the Power Council and the Power Outlaws were better off without him.

He thought maybe he was lying to himself, but he didn't want to think about that either.

That's when he noticed someone on the ground, waving wildly. It seemed to be a kid, but it was hard to tell. From up here they were the size of a grain of rice. The strange thing was that the rice-sized person seemed to be waving *at him*.

The last thing he wanted to do was go talk to some silly kid who wanted his autograph, but he was curious, so he dove for the ground, only letting his wings stop his fall when he was a few feet from crashing. He leveled out and landed softly. The person's mouth fell open. It was a kid, a young girl, around his age, with soft, brown skin and braided hair.

"Wow, it's you," the girl said. "You're him."

"Yes, usually I am myself," Axel said, suddenly wishing he'd stayed in the air. This was definitely an autograph-seeker. Ever since Nikki Powergloves fought Jimmy Powerboots in Cragglyville, the power kids had become sort of like celebrities.

The girl opened her mouth to speak again, but Axel raised a hand in the air. "I don't do autographs," he said.

"I don't want an autograph," she said, which surprised him. It also made him study her a bit more. He liked what she was wearing, from her leather jacket to her ripped up jeans to the skull and crossbones necklace. She looked pretty cool, emphasis on pretty.

"Then what *do* you want?" he asked.

"Your accent is so cool," she said.

"Uh, thanks," he said. "My father is from London. That's where I was born. We moved to the U.S. three years ago." *Why am I telling her all this?* he wondered to himself. He didn't even know her.

"Why weren't you at Niagara Falls?" the girl asked.

It was the last thing he expected her to say. It was none of her business what he did or where he went! "I was busy," he said.

"Too busy to be a hero?"

He pointed a finger at her. "Stay out of it."

"You're not scared of anyone," she said.

That wasn't exactly true. Axel was scared of people. He was scared of getting too close to them and then having to leave them behind. That's why he was a loner. "What do you know about me?"

The girl stepped forward. "I know they make fun of you on the base sometimes, because you never talk to anyone and eat alone. I know that you never back down or give them the satisfaction of knowing they've hurt your feelings. And now I know you're one of the power kids. I know that you're a hero."

"Stop saying that," Axel said. "I'm none of those things. I'm just a kid who wants to be left alone."

"Tough luck," the girl said, stepping even closer and sticking out her hand. "I'm Juniper, but my friends call me June."

Axel had no choice but to shake her hand. "Axel," he said. "I'll call you Juniper because we're not friends."

"Fine," she said. "Then I'll call you Axel Powerjackets because you're a superhero."

"I. Am. Not," Axel said, enunciating each word to get his point across.

"Well I am," June said. "Or at least I want to be. Consider me a hero in training. And I'll even be your sidekick for free, so long as you train me to be a hero."

Axel finally realized that this girl, June or Juniper or whatever, was completely nuts. "Well, nice meeting you, but I better get going." He started to pump his wings, but June raced forward and grabbed his legs with both arms, clinging to him tightly. "What are you doing?" Axel said. "Let go of me!"

"No," June said. "Either I'm your sidekick or I won't let go and you'll just have to fly with me hanging on the whole way."

Axel didn't know what to do. This girl was clearly a few tacos short of a Taco Bell, but he also didn't want her hanging on his legs all the time. "Fine," he said. "Whatever. It's not like being my sidekick means anything."

"Really? I can be your sidekick?" June asked, her rich, brown eyes lighting up.

"Yes. Yes." Axel waved his hand as if swatting a fly.

"Great!" June said, releasing his legs and offering her hand for a high-five. Axel ignored her, but then she said, "Are you going to leave me hanging?" so he slapped her palm. To his surprise, the high-five felt pretty good and he had to stop himself from smiling. He didn't want this girl to get the wrong idea.

"Okay then," Axel said. "I'll see you around."

"Wait!" June said, grabbing his hand. "We have our first mission."

Axel frowned. First mission? It dawned on him what she might mean. "Forget about it. I'm not going to Niagara Falls to help dig Nikki Powergloves out of the ice. Feel free to go yourself, Sidekick."

"We're not going to Niagara Falls," June said. "We're going to Italy."

6

Venice, Italy

Axel still couldn't believe he'd let Juniper talk him into using his powerbracelet to teleport them both to Italy. But it's not like he really had a choice. First Juniper showed him what was happening on the news, about the power kids that were in Italy. He'd groaned when he saw them. Naomi and Tyrone. He didn't really know Tyrone very well, but he seemed okay. Naomi, however, was a different story. She was a real pain in his rear end. She'd beaten him fair and square during the Great Adventure.

At first he hoped that Nikki and the Power Council would show up to fight Naomi and Tyrone, but then his powerbracelet had lit up and the gemstone in the center had turned a blue and red flannel color. Italy needed his help and Nikki and her friends must still be stuck under blocks of ice. He had to answer the call.

So after changing into his blue and red flannel jacket, he'd held Juniper's hand (which was really warm and smooth) and pressed the button on his powerbracelet. Now they were in Italy.

To be exact, they were in Venice, which was sort of like a floating city, crisscrossed with hundreds of canals. Because the roads were so narrow, the locals used the canals as the streets, travelling by boat, water taxi, or ferry. He'd been here before, when his parents were stationed in Europe.

They were in a large plaza full of people, vendors, and pigeons. There were so many pigeons that some of them were landing on the tourists so they could take bird pictures. In one corner of the plaza was an enormous church, built from stone, complete with beautiful arches and carvings. Four large stone horses guarded the plaza. Rising well above the church was a tall clock tower. Axel immediately recognized this place, from when his parents had brought him here. "Piazza San Marco," he murmured.

Juniper heard him and said, "What?"

"St. Mark's Square," he translated to English. "It's the main plaza in Venice. The locals call it 'La Piazza.'"

"Cool," Juniper said. "My dad was stationed in Rome once, but we never got to visit Venice."

"Well now you have," Axel said.

It was a warm summer's day and many of the locals and tourists were eating gelato, the Italian version of ice cream.

"I wish we had some Euros," Juniper complained. "I LOVE gelato."

Axel didn't want to tell her that he *did* have a Euro. It was his lucky coin, worth two Euros with gold in the center and silver around the edges. He always kept it in his pocket. "Yeah, me too," he lied, trying to keep a straight face. In truth, the gelato did look pretty good. A lady walked by licking a cone with his favorite flavor, *bacio*, which was chocolate hazelnut. His mouth watered and he licked his lips.

Focus, he reminded himself. *We're not here for sightseeing and ice cream. We have a mission.*

As if reading his mind, Juniper said, "There!" and pointed toward the top of the clock tower.

31

Axel craned his neck higher and higher, until he saw what she'd spotted. Or, more accurately, *who* she'd spotted. There was a massive creature hanging on the clock tower, its muscles bulging. The weirdest thing about the creature was that it had only one huge eye in the center of its forehead. Axel remembered learning about the mythical one-eyed creatures in school. They were called cyclops. And this cyclops was wearing a big gold watch. *Tyrone Powerbling*, Axel realized.

Next to Tyrone the Cyclops was a dark-haired girl wearing a purple skirt. It was Naomi, and she was laughing as Tyrone punched holes in the beautiful clock tower, raining down crumbling stones on the people below. The tourists and locals screamed, running for cover. Axel saw one man get hit by a brick and fall to the ground.

"Stay behind me," Axel said to Juniper. "I'll handle this."

"No way!" Juniper shouted, leaping past him. "I'm your sidekick, we're in this together!" Moving way faster than Axel expected, Juniper raced toward the clock tower, heading the opposite direction to the hordes of frightened people. Axel remembered a quote he had once heard his father talk about: *Heroes run toward danger when others run away.* So that either made Juniper a hero, or completely crazy. He was thinking crazy.

He took off after his sidekick, hoping he could catch up and protect her. Yeah, she was a little annoying, but he still didn't want to see her get hurt. As he ran, he used the power of his flannel jacket to transform into a gorilla, growing bigger and bigger and bigger, until the fleeing people started screaming because of him, and scattering like fallen leaves blown by the wind.

Soon Axel was so big that each stride was like three of Juniper's steps, even though he was running on all fours. He'd transformed into King Kong! When he passed his sidekick, she shouted, "Hey! Wait up!"

He ignored her and kept galloping. When he reached the base of the clock tower, he started climbing. As a gorilla, he was born to climb, easily finding handholds and footholds, using his feet just as well as his hands. Above him, Tyrone the Cyclops continued to rain down stone on his head, but the rubble just bounced off of his thick skin.

Naomi's eyes widened when she saw him getting closer, and she quickly climbed higher on the tower, using Tyrone as a shield. The one-eyed cyclops bellowed, and launched a huge rock at Axel's head, but he batted it away with a strong fist. Below him, he spotted Juniper, who jumped out of the way as the stone crashed to the plaza, shattering into a thousand pieces. "Stay back!" he tried to yell to her, but it came out as a roar.

Axel leaped higher, grabbing one of Tyrone's ankles and yanking him off the clock tower. The cyclops shrieked, trying to grab onto one of the holes he'd made in the tower, but it was too late, he was already falling. Tyrone flew through the air, his enormous arms wind-milling, but unfortunately for him, cyclops were unable to fly. Time seemed to move in slow motion as the creature fell, until he smashed onto the hard ground below, the earth shaking from the impact. The ground cracked and Tyrone lay still.

Once more, Axel roared, this time beating his chest with his fists while clinging to the tower with only his feet. He felt invincible!

"Hey you!" Naomi cried from above. He looked up. "Yeah, the big dumb monkey. You think you're so tough?"

Axel roared a response. He *did* think he was tough. Naomi Powerskirts didn't stand a chance against him.

That's when the world flipped upside down.

Suddenly, the tower was resting on its tip, and he was looking down instead of up. He felt himself sliding down the tower, which was really up, toward the sky, which was purple instead of blue. The clouds were green and the sun was black. Everything was all mixed up!

He'd underestimated Naomi and her purple skirt, which apparently had the power to mix up the world. He clutched at the stones, but his gorilla hands were no longer sticky, but slippery, sliding along the side of the building. He was falling into the sky. It made no sense, and yet he couldn't stop himself. His fingers left the building and he kept falling upwards, toward the purple sky and green clouds and black sun. With nothing to stop him, he would continue to fall forever and ever, until he went all the way into outer space!

Axel had never been so scared in his life. He didn't want to look at the weird mixed-up sky anymore, so he looked down at the upside-down tower. Naomi was staring up at him, laughing and shouting something about a big dumb monkey who thought he could fly.

But then he saw her. Juniper! His sidekick! She was gritting her teeth and climbing the upside-down tower with nothing more than her human hands and feet. She had a look of determination on her face, her eyes focused on Naomi. Naomi was too busy watching Axel fly away to notice her.

When Juniper reached Naomi, she grabbed her arms and pulled them behind her back, pinning her. Naomi flinched, surprised by the attack, and Axel immediately felt the world start to spin again. The sky turned blue, the clouds white, and the sun went from black to gold, shining down rays of warmth. Axel was still falling, but now he was tumbling back toward the tower, which was right side up.

As he was passing the tip, he reached out a gorilla arm and grabbed it, hanging on tightly. Below him, Juniper was struggling with Naomi, trying to fight her without tumbling from the tower. They were both starting to slip!

Axel leaped down the side of the tower with ease, scooping Naomi up with one hand and Juniper with the other. Once he had them both secure, he jumped, landing gracefully in the piazza. Nearby, Tyrone the Cyclops sat up, shaking his head.

"Let go of me!" Naomi shrieked, trying to pry Axel's ape fingers off of her.

"No way," Axel said, but again, it sounded just like a roar. He released Juniper and she climbed down, standing over Tyrone.

"That'll teach you to mess with Axel Powerjackets and his trusty sidekick, June the Goon," she said.

At that moment, a bright beam of light shot from Axel's closed fist and he felt Naomi disappear. When he opened his hand, she was gone, having escaped on a beam of light.

He quickly transformed back into himself. "Darn," he said. "She got away."

Juniper grinned. "That's okay. At least we got one of them."

Tyrone shrunk back down to his normal self, but before they could stop him, he'd opened his powerchest and switched his gold wristwatch for a gold pocket watch. An enormous black hole appeared and he said, "Later dudes," and stepped inside.

The hole closed in on itself and vanished, along with Tyrone.

"Double darn," Axel said.

"At least we saved Venice and the clock tower," Juniper said. "We were like real heroes, right?"

Axel couldn't help but to smile at his new sidekick. "*You* were a real hero, June," he said.

Juniper grinned back. "You called me June. Only my friends call me June."

Axel patted her on the back. "That's because you're my friend," he said. "June the Goon." It had a nice ring to it.

Before they left Venice, Axel used his lucky two-Euro coin to buy Juniper a gelato. "Bacio, my favorite!" she exclaimed when he gave it to her.

Axel sighed. It had been a weird, but good day. He'd made a surprising new friend in Juniper. She was a pretty good hero, too. He knew he still wasn't ready to join the Power Council, but at least he had someone to talk to.

7

Power kids attack the world

When Nikki woke up, she felt like she was covered in bruises.

Spencer was huddled over her, a worried expression on his face. Next to them was the big pile of ice blocks that Jimmy Powerboots had dumped on her. Nikki had never seen her old arch nemesis like that. He seemed so sad and angry. But that didn't mean he had to take it out on her! "Are you okay, Ice-Queen?" Spencer asked.

"I feel like a million bucks," Nikki said, grimacing in pain.

"Really?" Spencer asked.

"Yeah," Nikki said. "A million bucks that have been crumpled up, lit on fire, and then frozen into a big block of ashy ice."

"Very funny, Comedy-Central," Spencer said. "Let me help you up."

She took his offered hand and managed to get to her feet, aching all over. "Thanks for digging me out," Nikki said.

"It wasn't just me," Spence said. Right on cue, the rest of the Power Council huddled around her. They were all cold and wet, and Nikki remembered that some of them had been frozen, too. Beyond them, there were a dozen reporters and their crews with microphones and big cameras pointed at them. They all looked a little scared to come any closer, as if Nikki and her friends might bite them.

"Thanks guys," Nikki said. "I can't believe Jimmy beat me so badly."

Samantha stepped forward, her red belt crusted with icicles that were slowly melting, dripping water at her feet. "We all did our best, and we did really well. If not for Jimmy, we would've won."

"He seemed different," Nikki said.

"What do you mean?" Mike asked. His powerscarf was covered with flecks of ice.

"I don't know exactly," Nikki said. "He was more unpredictable. He seemed...sad." It was the only word she could think of to describe Jimmy just before he used his powers to break up all the ice.

"I felt like something weird was going on with all the Power Outlaws," Dexter said, his voice like a mouse. "It's like they were all fighting separately, instead of as a team. Like they don't really like each other very much."

They all stood in silence for a moment, thinking about what it could mean.

Eventually, Spencer said, "Nikki, there's something else we have to tell you. Something that's been happening while you were unconscious."

"What?" Nikki asked, noticing that all of the superheroes' powerbracelets were shining, including her own.

Instead of telling her, Spencer pulled out his iPad and showed it to her. The screen was split into four separate boxes, each showing a different news story. The headline at the top was "Power Kids Attack the World!"

"What the heck?" Nikki said. The box in the upper left was Niagara Falls, and showed the frozen falls and chunks of ice floating in the water. It was also playing a video of the fight between the Power Council and the Power Outlaws. *Ugh*, Nikki thought. *Now the whole world can watch the Power Outlaws beat us.*

But the other three boxes were showing different places. The upper right box showed a battle in Venice, Italy between Naomi and Tyrone, and a guy wearing a flannel jacket. "Axel!" Nikki exclaimed.

"Yeah," Spencer said, nodding excitedly. "We were trying to decide how to handle the situation in Italy when he showed up. And guess what? He has a sidekick!"

As the video rolled, Nikki could see that her own sidekick was right. The girl was fast, too, running right into danger, climbing a tower, and helping King Kong Axel defeat Naomi Powerskirts.

"I didn't think he had it in him," Samantha said. "But I'm glad he did."

"Maybe he's not so bad after all," Freddy agreed. Coming from Freddy, that was saying a lot. Since the moment he met the English power kid, Axel had teased Freddy about being overweight.

Nikki continued to scan the iPad screen. At the bottom there were two more boxes, each with news from a different place. The first was in Egypt, where Tanya Powershirts and Sue Powerslippers were standing outside King Tut's tomb screaming at tourists. Every once and a while Sue would yell, "Come and get us, Power Council! Or are you too scared?"

The final box was labeled "Mount Kilimanjaro, Africa." The whir of a helicopter droned in the background, and a reporter said, "The child supervillain known as Peter Powerhats has been threatening to 'bring down the mountain' if at least one member of the child superhero group known as the Power Council doesn't show up. There are also rumors that the original Power Outlaw, Jimmy Powerboots, is in the area."

"Oh gosh," Nikki said. "I've got to get to that mountain right now!"

Samantha stepped forward and put a hand on Nikki's shoulder. "We decided that me, Freddy and our sidekicks are going to go to Mount Kilimanjaro."

"What? No," Nikki said, shaking her head. "This is my fault. I lost to Jimmy. I have to stop him."

"None of this is your fault, Nick-Nack," Spencer said. "Listen to Samantha, she knows what she's talking about."

Nikki turned back toward Samantha and waited. "They're expecting you to go to fight Jimmy. It's what they want. That's why you can't go. You and Spence have to go with Britney to Egypt, to that tomb. Mike will get back to the Power City to monitor the situation, and he'll come to help us if we need him."

She knew her friend was right. Samantha had been the leader of the Power Council for longer than Nikki had even been a superhero. She trusted her to make the right decisions. "Okay," she said, opening her powerchest. The other kids already had theirs open. "Choose your powers!"

She and Spence huddled over her powerbracelet, which was showing a glove that was half-red and half-orange. "Super-speed and fire!" Spencer yelled as Nikki quickly removed the gloves she was wearing and replaced them with one orange and one red one.

After closing the lid on her powerchest, Nikki watched it shrink down and then pocketed it. When she turned to Britney, she found her friend trying to fasten a new pair of earrings, but her hands were shaking so much she couldn't seem to do it. "It's going to be okay," Nikki said, inspecting the earrings. They were clear crystals, sparkling under the sunlight. Diamonds! "Wow, these are beautiful," Nikki said.

"Thanks," Britney said. Her hands finally stopped shaking and she poked the earrings through each of her pierced ears, clasping them at the back. When she finished, her fingers automatically went to her ears, feeling the diamonds. "I don't know if I can do this," she said. "That last fight, it was—"

"You were amazing," Nikki said. "You threw those mini-discs like a champ, Britney. You were every bit as good as the rest of us."

"Really?"

The rest of the Power Council and the sidekicks huddled around her, agreeing. "We wouldn't have done nearly as well if you hadn't taken out Tyrone," Spencer said. "You were awesome!"

"Thanks," Britney said, smiling. "It's just—I've never been good at something before."

"Well you're good at being a hero," Freddy said.

"You'll be fine," Samantha said. "You, Nikki and Spencer will be there for each other."

"We should get going," Nikki said, feeling the familiar thrill in her gut that she always got before a battle.

Spencer grabbed her hand. "To the tomb!" he cried.

Nikki knew Sue and Tanya would be a hard fight, but with her friends by her side she knew they could win.

8

King Tut's Tomb, Egypt

King Tut's Tomb was a big mound of rock flanked by sheer cliffs that rose toward a clear sky. The bright yellow sun was so hot it seemed to roar with dragon fire.

"It's like we're standing in a campfire," Spencer pointed out. "Hot tamales!"

Nikki remembered the last time she was in Egypt, for the Great Adventure. The challenge was to cover the Great Pyramid in chocolate while fighting off Tyrone Powerbling, who'd grown as large as a Greek god. With Spencer's help they'd managed to win. Something told her this fight would be much harder.

Britney appeared beside them, still playing with her earrings. Except now she was a human diamond! Her entire body sparkled under the harsh sunlight. A group of tourists standing nearby *oohed* and *ahhed* and started snapping photographs. When Britney moved, her diamond body moved with her, like it was a liquid. But when Nikki reached out to grab her friend's arm, she found that her skin was as hard as steel. Spencer touched Britney's other arm. "Wow!" they both said together.

Britney said, "When I'm in diamond form, I don't think anything can hurt me." That thought seemed to give her strength. Truthfully, it made Nikki feel stronger too.

"Great," Nikki said. She wanted to say more, but before she could, a sugar-sweet voice called out.

"Oh Nikki Powergloves! Come on in to our little house of horrors! Unless you're too scared?" Sue Powerslippers was standing in the shadow of the tomb's entrance, looking as beautiful as always, her Barbie-hair falling perfectly to her shoulders. Nikki's gaze fell to Sue's slippers, which were black. They looked to be made out of some kind of rough material. *Snakeskin*, Nikki thought, wondering what terrible power the slippers gave Sue.

Tanya Powershirts stood next to her, looking uncomfortable in a black and white t-shirt. There was a picture of a mummy on it. It had no mouth and only black holes for eyes. Nikki shuddered, which only made Tanya grin a crooked-toothed grin.

Then the two Power Outlaws vanished inside the tomb.

"Are we really going to follow them in there?" Britney said, sounding scared again.

"I don't think we have a choice," Nikki said. "If we don't, they might destroy the whole tomb and hurt someone. Spence, what do you know about King Tut's Tomb?" Having a genius best friend was almost the same as having a friend named Google.

Spencer cleared his throat. "I think the tomb was discovered almost a hundred years ago. It was full of treasure, but they moved most of it to some museum for safe-keeping. It's the tomb of a really young Egyptian pharaoh, named Tutankhamun, but most people just call him King Tut for short. He was only nine when he became pharaoh, and died ten years later."

"Wait wait wait," Britney said. "This is some teenager's tomb? As in, there's a dead guy in there?" Despite the desert heat, Nikki suddenly felt very cold. She remembered the mummy on Tanya's shirt.

"Yes, his mummy's still in the tomb," Spencer said.

Nikki grabbed Britney's diamond-hard hand before she had time to freak out. "We'll be fine," Nikki said. "You're as strong as a diamond, remember?"

"Strong as a diamond, strong as a diamond," Britney said, sparkling with every word.

Nikki pulled her friend toward the tomb with Spencer trailing behind. Just before they reached the mountain of stone, Nikki noticed two Weebles sitting on top. One was black and one was white. "Yin," the white one said. "Yang," the black one answered. Nikki didn't know what to think about the strange Oreo-colored Weebles that were following her around, but she didn't have time to figure it out right now. She turned her attention back to her mission.

The entrance to the tomb was full of shadows, but just beyond was a staircase lit from above. Nikki ran one hand along the stone walls as they descended. Spencer counted the steps as they went. He liked counting, something about it helped calm his nerves. "One, two, three," he counted. Their footsteps echoed in the tunnel ahead of them. Nikki stepped off the last step and a few seconds later Spencer said, "FIFTEEN!" *Fifteen, fifteen, fifteen, fifteen!* his voice echoed.

Everything went quiet, except for the scrape of their footsteps. It was so quiet Nikki could hear her own breathing and the beat of her heart. Every second, Nikki expected Sue to attack, but she didn't. They kept walking, and the tunnel angled downwards, until they passed through a doorway. Nikki gasped. The chamber they entered was much bigger than the tunnel, and had beautiful drawings of Egyptians on the walls. But that's not what made Nikki gasp.

To the right was a stone coffin. The tomb of King Tut's mummy.

"I feel like we should bow or something," Spencer said. "All hail King Tut, boy pharaoh!"

That's when the attack came. Not from in front of them, where the coffin was, but from the side, where a small room connected to the main burial chamber.

They lurched out in pairs, their arms outstretched like zombies, dragging tattered white bandages.

"Mummies!" Spencer yelled, trying to run.

But it was too late. One of the mummies had already grabbed Spencer by the back of his shirt. Cloth-covered fingers clawed at his shoulders.

"No!" Britney shouted, charging the mummies. Nikki had never seen anything so brave in her life, as she watched Diamond-Britney bash into the mummy, knocking it away from Spencer. The mummy went flying, but three more immediately replaced it, trying to grab Britney. In her diamond form, she seemed to be invincible, knocking them back again and again, as Nikki helped Spencer to his feet. Britney was singlehandedly defeating the mummies!

But then Sue appeared, rising from behind King Tut's coffin like a ghost. "Did you miss me?" she asked, but before Nikki could answer, Sue blinked her eyes twice and a gray blob shot out.

"Look out!" Nikki yelled, pulling Spencer down to the ground. The gray orb flew past them and collided with Britney, who was still fighting the mummies. The girl spun around, looking for who hit her. Nikki noticed that the gray blob was growing bigger, covering Britney's entire body, replacing the diamond.

"What...is....happening.....to......me?" Britney said, each word slower than the last. Her arms turned gray, then her legs, her stomach, her neck, and finally her face, until she couldn't talk anymore. She had turned into stone!

Sue was laughing now, and, because of the way it echoed, it sounded like there were a dozen Sues all around them. Without Diamond-Britney to stop them, the mummies charged once more. Without thinking, Nikki pushed Spencer back into the tunnel and began shooting balls of fire from her fingertips. The dry cloth covering each mummy's body easily caught on fire. Mummy after mummy began to disappear, vanishing as if they never existed at all.

Using her super-speed glove, Nikki raced forward into the side room and tackled Tanya, who was creating another mummy, her hands full of white bandages. In a flash, Nikki had wrapped the bandages all around Tanya's body, until she couldn't move. She even covered her mouth so the girl couldn't speak, and her eyes so she couldn't see. She left a small gap so Tanya could breathe out of her nose.

Less than three seconds had passed, and Nikki had captured one of the Power Outlaws.

But she wasn't done yet. Sue was still laughing in the tomb, and Nikki knew that one hit from one of Sue's gray globs would turn her to stone.

She sprinted through the doorway so fast she was only a blur. Sue started blinking rapidly, gray globs bursting from her eyes, filling the air like rain. Nikki was like lightning, dodging the gray globs, ducking, jumping, and fighting her way toward the Power Outlaw, who continued to blink furiously.

Faster than a bullet, Nikki jammed both hands onto King Tut's coffin and vaulted it, narrowly missing one of Sue's gray globs. She crashed into her, knocking her backwards against one of the painted stone walls. "Oww!" Sue cried out, tumbling away.

Nikki was on her feet in an instant, pinning Sue to the ground on her stomach. The girl struggled against her, trying to turn her head so she could blink at her, but Nikki was stronger. "It's over, Sue," Nikki said. "You lost."

"It's never over," Sue growled, still fighting to push Nikki off. "I just heard that Jimmy and Peter BEAT your other friends over at Mount Kilimanjaro."

Nikki froze. It couldn't be true, could it? Samantha, Freddy and their sidekicks would never lose to Jimmy and Peter. As she was thinking about it, Nikki lost her concentration, relaxing her muscles slightly. Sue was ready for it, twisting away, immediately jamming her finger on her powerbracelet. She smiled a beautiful, evil smile and disappeared.

"Shoot!" Nikki said. She'd been fooled and Sue had escaped.

"Hey, Flash!" Spencer shouted. "You okay?"

Nikki didn't feel okay, but she wasn't hurt. "I'm fine," she said, heading back toward her friends. Spencer was peeking around the doorway, making sure it was safe. "Sue got away."

"That's okay," Spence said. "The important thing is that we're all safe."

Britney was curled up in a ball, her body once more made of diamonds. She was sobbing. Nikki and Spencer crouched down next to her and helped her up. "You're okay now," Nikki said.

"It felt like I was being buried alive," Britney explained. Instead of tears, small diamonds tumbled from her eyes, bouncing to the floor.

"Remind me never to get hit by one of Sue's gray globs," Spencer said.

Nikki gave her sidekick a look that said *You're not helping!* Then she said, "Don't worry. We still won. You saved us from the mummies and then I saved you from Sue's stone globs. That's the way a team works. We help each other."

Britney nodded, but she still looked so sad. She was the saddest diamond Nikki had ever seen. "It wasn't even the stone," she said. "I thought I was going to lose you guys. I can't lose my friends. I practically just met you."

"You won't," Nikki promised. She gave her friend a hug and Spencer joined in.

There was a groan from the other room, and they quickly pulled apart. "More mummies?" Spencer asked. Britney put her diamond fists up, ready for another fight.

"Just one," Nikki said, grinning. "And her name is Tanya Powershirts."

Nikki led the way, and then they stood around the captured Power Outlaw. Tanya was rolling around, trying to get loose. She'd managed to make a hole for one eye, which stared out at them. "Lemme outta here!" she said, her voice muffled through the cloth.

"Why should we?" Spencer said. "You attacked us with your mummies."

The cloth above Tanya's lips moved. "I dinnit illy unt to."

"What was that?" Nikki asked, moving one of the bandages so Tanya could speak.

"I didn't really want to," Tanya said.

It's not what Nikki expected her to say. "Why should we believe you?" Spencer asked. "You joined the Power Outlaws. You could've joined the Power Council."

Tanya the Mummy shook her head. "I couldn't," she said. "You'd never take me."

"What?" Nikki said. "Of course we would. Anyone that wants to be a superhero and help do good in the world is welcome to join us."

"Except me," Tanya said.

Nikki didn't understand. Clearly, she was missing something. She shook her head. "Including you," she said.

"I'm too…ugly," Tanya said. "No one except bad kids want to hang around with me. And even the bad kids make fun of me. Just before you guys showed up, Sue was calling me Freak-Face."

Nikki could picture Sue in her head. The way she would laugh at Tanya, tossing her perfect blond hair and batting her perfect eyelashes. It made her sick and angry. "We're not like that," Nikki said. "Tell her, Britney."

Britney seemed startled that Nikki was asking her opinion. "She's t-telling the t-truth," she stammered.

"No one's perfect," Spencer explained. "Freddy's overweight and Dexter is too short and Britney cries too much—sorry Britney—and Samantha is too bossy and Nikki is—"

"Watch it, Mister," Nikki said, cutting him off. "And Spencer is too smart for his own good sometimes."

"True," Spencer agreed. "And I'm a big nerd." He peeled back the bandages until they could see the rest of Tanya's face.

Tanya frowned an ugly frown. "And I'm more hideous than a warty toad," she said.

"No," Nikki said, shaking her head. "Your teeth are a little crooked, so what? Nothing braces won't fix when you're older. And your eyes are a little crossed, big deal! You probably just need glasses."

"And my big, stupid, crooked nose?" Tanya said.

"You'll grow into it," Spencer said, taking over. "The most important thing is what's in your heart. Do you want to be bad or good?"

Tanya bit her lip, thinking it over for a minute. "Good," she finally said. "I want to be good. I feel awful when I do bad things."

"Then you're officially a member of the Power Council," Nikki said. "And you've got eight new friends now. Plus all the Weebles, which is like a million."

Tanya smiled, she actually smiled. And for the first time since Nikki had met her, Tanya looked kind of pretty. "You should smile more often," Nikki said. "You're really pretty when you do."

9

Mount Kilimanjaro, Africa

Jimmy Powerboots was happy to be back alongside Peter Powerhats. They didn't need all those other Power Outlaws. Things were better when it was just him and Peter fighting against Nikki Powergloves. Things were easier then. Simpler.

"We should bring down the whole mountain," Peter said. He was taller than Jimmy, casting a shadow over him as they both stared up toward the rocky peak of Mount Kilimanjaro. According to some book he'd once read, Mount Kilimanjaro was the largest free-standing mountain in the world, almost 20,000 feet high! It was even an active volcano that could erupt at any second. Jimmy thought that was pretty cool.

But he didn't think bringing down the whole mountain would be very cool. "I don't know..." Jimmy said. "A lot of people could get hurt."

"Since when do you care about hurting people?" Peter asked.

Jimmy thought about it. It had been a long time since he'd cared about anything other than trying to get Nikki to join his side. After all, that was why he started fighting with her in the first place. He just wanted to be her friend. But she had her own friends now. She didn't need Jimmy. "Maybe I'm just tired of destroying things," he said. Even as he said it, Jimmy was shocked at himself. He used to *love* destroying things. It was one of his favorite things to do. But not anymore. He still felt awful about breaking all that ice and dumping it on Nikki's head. If he could take it back, he would. That got him thinking about the special device he was working on. As soon as it was finished, he was planning to use it against *all* of the power kids, not just the Power Council. He was going to change the game forever.

He realized Peter was laughing at him. "You're weird," Peter said, still laughing.

Jimmy had always been a bit weird. The kids at school never got his jokes, and when he tried to talk to them they would pretend not to hear him. Sometimes it made him angry, but mostly it just made him sad. Sue and Naomi reminded him of the kids at school.

Wanting to change the subject, Jimmy said, "We should get ready. The Power Council could be here at any second."

"I was born ready," Peter said. He was wearing a peach colored hat with a picture of a big hand on it. The moment he spoke, his own two hands began to grow. And grow. And grow and grow and grow! They grew until they were like a giant's hands, so big he could probably pick up a car with them. Maybe even a truck.

Jimmy looked down at his boots. One was black and one was white. Kind of like those two Weebles he saw looking at Nikki Powergloves through the pile of ice. What were those Weebles doing at Niagara Falls anyway?

He shook his head, trying to concentrate on his white boot. The black one he would use later, but the white one he could use right now. So he did.

A second Jimmy appeared, then a third. Two more popped into existence, appearing from the thin mountain air. One of them said, "Hi, Jimmy," and another said, "What's up, Jimmy?" It was kind of weird talking to his clones. They were just like him in every way, even wearing the same black and white boots. Recently he'd learned that his clones could make their own clones if he asked them to.

"Clone yourself," he said to the other four Jimmys. So they did. Each clone made four other clones, until there were twenty-one Jimmys, including him. "Again," he said, and then there were more clones, one-hundred-and-one to be exact. "Again. Again. Again." He kept repeating himself, until there were so many Jimmys he couldn't even count them anymore.

All the Jimmys were talking at once, saying "Hi, Jimmy," and "What's up, Jimmy?" over and over again. Some were climbing on Peter's big hands and he was carrying them around. The mountain was covered with Jimmys!

Now Jimmy had lots of friends, he didn't need Nikki Powergloves or anyone else.

"There!" Peter shouted, waving his giant hands over his head to get Jimmy's attention. He pointed a huge finger down the mountainside.

The rest of the Jimmys started pointing and yelling, "There! There!"

Jimmy craned his neck to see over them. Two members of the Power Council had appeared on the mountain. But not Nikki. His heart sank. He was really hoping Nikki would come. He wanted to apologize for dumping all the ice on her head. He hoped she wasn't hurt.

Instead it was Samantha Powerbelts and Freddy Powersocks, along with their two sidekicks. Samantha was wearing a bright orange belt. Jimmy couldn't see what kind of socks Freddy was wearing. Even though Jimmy had cloned himself a zillion times, the Power Council didn't look scared at all.

They charged!

"Get them!" Peter yelled, slapping his ginormous hands together with a *SLAP!* that sounded like the crack of a whip.

Jimmy wished he was somewhere else, somewhere he could just hang out with his clones and play baseball, or videogames. He didn't want to be here. He didn't feel like fighting. But he had no choice. If he didn't fight, the Power Council would hurt him.

"Powerstomp!" he shouted, which was the power of the black boot he and his clones were wearing. In unison, every single Jimmy stomped their feet. The impact was so powerful that it actually shook the mountain, sounding like the crack of thunder. The ground opened up, splitting as easily as a piece of string cheese being ripped in half. A bunch of Jimmys fell in the hole and disappeared, but it didn't matter—Jimmy could always make more clones.

The earthquake Jimmy had created also made some boulders rumble down the hill. Some of his Jimmys were knocked over, but not him. He ducked and dodged, letting them roll past him, breaking into a million pieces.

Peter was using his giant hands to catch the boulders and then launch them toward the Power Council. One of them flew toward Samantha, but suddenly ropes shot out from her hands and wrapped around the stone. She spun in a circle, swinging the heavy rock and then releasing it. The boulder soared through the air, right at Peter. Peter managed to catch it with his big hands, but the force of it knocked him backwards. The stone landed on top of Peter, trapping him.

Freddy started using his own power to burrow beneath the mountain, creating tunnels. Jimmy's clones chased him into the caves, but then Freddy popped back out and the tunnels collapsed on the Jimmys' heads.

One of the sidekicks, the amateur magician named Chilly, pulled out a black top hat. When she threw it into the air, a whole flock of white doves burst out, and started attacking more of Jimmy's clones, pecking at them as they ran down the mountain.

The other sidekick, a short Asian kid named Dexter, used a water pistol to shoot some kind of liquid all over the mountain. Jimmy remembered that same liquid being used against him before. "Watch out!" he yelled to his clones, but it was too late. The Sticky Situation

Glue had already stuck a bunch of his clones to the ground. They were trying to lift their legs but couldn't. "Hey!" they yelled. "Hey! Hey! Hey!"

Samantha was still fighting hard, too, shooting ropes in every direction, tying up the Jimmys.

Jimmy hated what was happening, hated watching all his clones get hurt, hated seeing Peter trapped under the boulder. He felt dizzy watching the fight. He knew he should be doing something, powerstomping or creating more clones, but all he wanted to do was get out of there and go back to working on his device.

He ran toward Peter, but the huge crack in the ground was blocking him. It was too wide for him to leap over, so he looked for another way across. There was a massive boulder that had gotten wedged in the crack. Some of his clones were climbing over it, crossing to the other side. He joined them, clambering up the rough boulder to the top.

That's when the boulder started to crack in the middle.

He froze, trying to keep his balance. Beneath the boulder was a mouth of darkness, waiting to eat him. If he fell, he was done for!

The thin crack became a bigger crack and finally a full split. The boulder broke into two pieces, tumbling into the chasm. Jimmy fell, screaming as the black surrounded him.

Until he stopped, his body bouncing up and down. Something long and rough had wrapped around him, stopping his fall. Ropes. Lots of long, orange ropes. His eyes followed them until they reached Samantha's hands and then her face. She was wearing a determined expression and slowly pulling the ropes back up. Jimmy felt his body being lifted out of the hole.

When his feet hit solid ground again, the ropes slithered away like snakes, back to Samantha. "You okay?" she asked.

Why was she asking Jimmy whether he was okay? She was supposed to be his enemy. Right? He wasn't sure. She'd saved his life. "Yeah. Thank you," was all he managed to say.

"We won," Samantha said. "Get out of here."

"You mean, you're going to let us go?" Jimmy asked, shocked. Was it really going to be this easy to escape?

"Yes. But don't forget what I did for you," Samantha said.

"I—I won't." Jimmy snapped his fingers and all of his clones vanished into whatever weird Clone World they'd come from. Jimmy ran over to Peter, who was still stuck under the rock. He switched to his yellow boots, so he could teleport, then grabbed Peter's hand and transported them back to the warehouse.

Standing there next to Big-Hands Peter, Jimmy remembered how Samantha had saved him. It almost felt like a dream. *Don't forget what I did for you*, she'd said. *I won't*, he thought. *I'll never forget.*

Jimmy smiled. He couldn't remember the last time he'd smiled.

But then Naomi, Tyrone, and Sue appeared beside them. Naomi looked like she wanted to punch him, Tyrone's face was so mad Jimmy thought he might eat him, and Sue was so angry she was literally hopping up and down with her fists balled at her sides.

Jimmy's smile vanished. Then he realized Tanya was missing.

10

Voting on Tanya

They were back in the Power City eating pizza and watching the news. Nikki was on her fifth slice. Fighting bad guys always made her really hungry. What a day it had been!

Axel and his new mysterious sidekick had defeated Naomi and Tyrone, Nikki, Britney and Spencer had beaten Sue and Tanya, and she'd just watched the video of Samantha, Freddy, and their two sidekicks taking down Jimmy's clones and Peter. All of the battles were pretty amazing!

Tanya was sitting by herself in the corner. She was wearing a lime green shirt with green gobs of slime drawn all over it. Freddy and Mike seemed scared to look at her, Dexter and Chilly had positioned themselves all the way on the other side of the room as if she might have cooties, and Spencer wouldn't stop staring at her. Britney kept smiling at Tanya, but Tanya never smiled back.

"Are you sure she's not a spy?" Samantha whispered to Nikki.

Nikki thought about it. Tanya didn't seem like a spy. She seemed like a shy, scared girl who needed some friends. "I really don't think she's a spy," Nikki whispered back. "She even smiled when I told her she could be a member of the Power Council."

"She's not smiling now," Samantha pointed out.

It was true. Tanya looked like the girl Nikki remembered from before. The girl with the strange frowning face. Luckily, they had a secret weapon when people were sad.

"Tanya," Nikki said.

Tanya looked up, her crossed eyes wide with surprise. Her mouth opened, but she didn't speak, as if her words were stuck on her tongue.

Nikki stood up and crossed the room, standing next to Tanya. "Did you get enough pizza?" Nikki asked. "Because Mike can always make some more. You can have any toppings you like."

"Uh. Thanks. I'm full. Maybe later." Tanya was staring at her hands.

"You don't have to be afraid of us," Nikki said.

"I'm not!" Tanya said, looking up. "It's just…people don't usually like me very much. And your sidekick looks like he wants to do experiments on me."

Nikki glanced at Spencer, who was still staring at Tanya. "Spence. Cut it out! You're making our newest member uncomfortable."

"Oh," Spence said, as if just realizing he'd been staring. "Sorry. I was just wondering what power that shirt gives you. Slime power?"

Tanya looked down at her shirt. "Yeah," she said. "I can shoot slime in all different ways, like slime bullets and slime spray. I can even make slime rain."

"Awesome!" Spencer exclaimed. Nikki saw Tanya's lips twitch, like she really wanted to smile. But she didn't. It was time for the secret weapon.

"Hey, do you want to go to Weebleville and meet the Weebles?" Nikki asked her.

"Uh…" Tanya said.

"Great idea, Braniac!" Spencer said. "We have to give her all the Weeble rules too."

"Rules?" Tanya said, finally making eye contact with Spencer. Curiosity gleamed in her eyes.

Spencer raised one finger. "One—never pet the Weebles. They are NOT pets."

"Okay," Tanya said.

Spencer lifted a second finger. "Two—don't accuse the Weebles of lying, even when they say something crazy. Everything they say is the truth."

"Okay," Tanya said.

"Finally, three," Spencer said, raising his third finger. "Never—I repeat, NEVER—feed the Weebles after midnight. I learned all about this one the hard way."

"Why? What happened?" Tanya asked. Nikki was glad Tanya was finally starting to talk.

Spencer grinned. "The little Weeble turned into Godzilla Weeble and almost destroyed the whole place."

Tanya's eyes grew huge. "Wow! Really?"

Spencer got up and took Tanya's hand, pulling her in the direction of Weebleville. "Yeah, it was kind of scary, but mostly awesome," he said. "I'll tell you the whole story on the way there." Chilly and Dexter followed after them.

Nikki started to follow her sidekick, but Mike stopped her. "Huddle," he said. Samantha and Freddy crowded around them. Mike said, "This is a very bad idea. Tanya is one of *them*. She's a Power Outlaw."

"No she's not," Nikki said. "Not anymore. She's one of us."

Mike shook his head. "We don't even know her."

Nikki laughed at that. "Don't you remember when you met me and Spence? We didn't know you guys either, and you didn't know us."

"That was different," Mike said.

"How?"

"We'd been watching you fight Jimmy. You were one of the good guys."

"Tanya is too," Nikki said. "She just got involved with some bad kids because she thought we wouldn't like her. It's not her fault. She wants to help us."

"We should vote," Mike said. "It's only fair."

Samantha nodded. "He's right."

Nikki sighed. She didn't like where this was going. "Fine," she said. "I vote yes."

Mike immediately said, "No way, Jose."

Freddy looked at Nikki with his dark brown eyes. "Sorry," he said. "I don't trust her. No."

Nikki wanted to get down on her knees and beg Samantha to say yes. But instead she just looked at the leader of the Power Council. If Samantha said no, Tanya would be kicked out. If Samantha said yes, it would be 2-2 and Samantha's vote as the leader would be the tiebreaker. Tanya would get to stay.

"Yes," Samantha said. A grin exploded on Nikki's face and she wanted to hug their leader. Samantha said, "Mike, Freddy, I know why you guys feel the way you do toward Tanya. She did some bad things. She hung out with some bad kids. But that doesn't make her bad on the inside. She *wants* to be here. She *wants* to help us. She deserves a second chance."

Mike didn't seem happy, but he nodded. Freddy nodded too.

"Thank you," Nikki said. "You won't regret this."

11

Auditioning villain sidekicks

"Forget about Freak-Face," Sue said. "We don't need her anyway."

"She has a name," Tyrone said, clenching his teeth. "Her name is Tanya. And we do need her. Now the Power Council has six heroes and we only have five villains. Plus they have all those sidekicks. We're outnumbered."

Jimmy was sitting against the wall working on his special device. He was listening to the argument about Tanya and wondering how she managed to join the Power Council. He wondered whether she was happier with Nikki and her friends. *Would I be happier with them, too?* he asked himself.

"We could try to recruit Axel and his sidekick," Naomi suggested.

Tyrone nodded in agreement. "Yeah! They were really tough to beat."

"That punk is a loser," Sue said. "He'll never join anyone."

"We didn't have any other choice," Naomi said. "Tyrone is right. We need more Power Outlaws if we're going to win."

"I got it!" Peter said, surprising everyone. He was wearing his orange baseball cap and burping fireballs at the metal warehouse wall. There was a big black spot where the fire had burned the metal. "We could break into all the prisons in the world and help the prisoners escape! Yeah! Then they would have to join us. *BURP!*" Another fireballs burst from his mouth and slammed into the wall.

Naomi rolled her eyes. "That's the dumbest idea I've ever heard. Those criminals are all adults. They would try to tell us what to do and act like we're stupid kids."

"But we are stupid kids," Peter said, burping another fireball.

"No," Naomi said. "We're *special*. We're better than ALL the other kids. We could rule this world if we could beat the Power Losers."

"Don't you mean the Power Council?" Jimmy said, finally looking up.

"Did I say you could talk?" Naomi said, glaring at him.

Jimmy dropped his head and went back to working on his secret project. He was almost finished.

"We need sidekicks," Sue said. "That's the only way we can make this a fair fight."

Jimmy looked up again. All the other kids were nodding in agreement. "How do we get them?" he asked. Jimmy had always wanted a sidekick, but never knew how to find one.

"Duh," Sue said, as if it was the stupidest question in the world. "We hold Villain Sidekick Auditions."

Sue and Naomi agreed that Peter and Tyrone would be the best kids to recruit for them, so they sent the two boys out to find some potential sidekicks.

Jimmy sat by himself, wishing he was somewhere else, while Naomi and Sue argued about everything. He stayed quiet, afraid to get in the middle of it. The only thing that kept Jimmy from running out the door was his little project. The device was nearly perfect. He just needed to add a few more wires and connect everything together. If not for his red/blue/yellow boots, he never would've been able to build the complicated machine.

While Jimmy was still working, Peter and Tyrone returned with some possible sidekicks. There were about ten of them, five girls and five boys. They all looked pretty mean and one of the girls even had a black eye.

"Do you know who we are?" Naomi asked them.

The biggest guy, a boy with pale, freckled skin and big blue eyes said, "Duh, you're the Power Outlawsh. You're all over the newsh. You've been deshtroying thingsh everywhere." He slobbered when he talked, drool dripping from his mouth.

Naomi smiled. Jimmy could tell she liked being famous. Jimmy used to like being famous, but not anymore. "That's right. And what do you think about what we're doing?"

The boy said, "I think it'sh cool and I want to help!" More slobber. More drool.

"How can you help?" Sue asked. "Do you have any skills besides spraying spit everywhere when you talk?"

The guy grinned. "I'm Dante Jamesh, but my friendsh call me Shlobber."

"I wonder why…" Naomi said sarcastically. Jimmy felt kind of bad for the kid. It wasn't his fault he had a speech impediment.

"It'sh becaushe I shlobber a lot," Slobber said, not getting that she was making fun of him. "Anywaysh, I'm really shtrong and I can throw thingsh really far. I'm the quarterback on my football team."

"Let's see it," Sue said. Slobber just happened to have a football in his hand, as if he never left home without it.

"What should I throw it at?" Slobber asked.

"Hey, Jimmy!" Sue said. Jimmy flinched. He didn't expect her to say his name. "You should run across the warehouse."

"Run?" Jimmy said, not realizing what she was talking about.

"Yeah, show these morons how fast you are," Sue said.

Jimmy shrugged. He *was* pretty fast. He stood up, glanced at the ten kids, and then took off. He bolted across the wide warehouse, his legs moving faster and faster.

"Hit him," he heard Sue say from across the room.

He didn't even have time to think about what she meant before he heard the whistling in the air and felt the thump of the football hitting him in the back of the head. It knocked him forward and he fell, scraping his hands and knees on the concrete. "Oomf!" he said, the air leaving his lungs.

He lay there for a moment, trying to breath, watching blood trickle from the scrapes on his knees. His hands were stinging.

Across the warehouse, Naomi said, "Nice arm, Slobber. Stand over there. Who wants to try out next?"

Jimmy managed to roll over and sit up, his ears still ringing from when the football hit his head. Slobber was grinning a sloppy grin at him from across the room.

Sue is SO mean, he thought. *I'm supposed to be one of her allies, and she doesn't even care if I get hurt?* Jimmy knew if it wasn't for his powers at Niagara Falls, they would've lost. No one seemed to appreciate him anymore, except maybe Peter.

While Jimmy was feeling sorry for himself, the Villain Sidekick Auditions continued. There was one girl who could stand on her head for a really long time. Jimmy thought that was sort of cool, but he wasn't sure how it would help them fight against the Power Council. One of the boys could juggle. Another could scream really really loud. Naomi told him if he ever did that again, she'd seal his mouth with super glue. There was also an interesting girl who called herself Weasel. She had short blond hair and gray-colored eyes. Her "skill" was stealing stuff, which Jimmy knew wasn't a very nice thing to do. But Weasel was very good at it. Before they knew what hit them, Weasel had stolen stuff from half the other kids. Naomi and Sue seemed impressed, too.

The last possible sidekick was another girl. She had brown skin, brown eyes, and dark hair. Jimmy thought she was really pretty, not that he'd ever admit it out loud.

"What's your name and what can you do?" Naomi asked.

The girl smiled a big smile and Jimmy was surprised to see that two of her teeth stuck out on each side and looked really sharp, almost like fangs. "My name is Shakti Shahari, but people call me Sharkey."

"Because of the teeth?" Sue asked.

"Yes," Sharkey said.

"What can you do?" Naomi asked.

"Bite stuff."

Jimmy frowned. *Bite stuff?* She looked to be at least nine years old. Most kids stopped biting when they were really little.

"Show me," Naomi said, glancing at Jimmy.

Oh no! Jimmy thought. *Not me!* He started to back up, sliding on his butt across the floor.

But Naomi looked away from Jimmy and said, "Bite the screamer."

The kid who had screamed really loud tried to run for the door, but Slobber grabbed him and picked him up by the collar of his shirt. "Going somewhere?" he said.

"Please," the screamer said. "Lemme go. I want to go home to my mommy!" He kicked and squirmed and tried to get free, but Slobber held him tightly.

Sharkey skipped over, a big smile on her face. "This might hurt just a little," she said. Then she bit him on the leg.

"Ahhhh!" the screamer screamed. "My leg!"

Sharkey pulled back, grinning a shark-like grin. Even from across the warehouse, Jimmy could see the teeth marks on the screamer's leg. Slobber released the poor boy and he ran from the warehouse crying.

"Do you think you can bite Nikki Powergloves the way you bit the screamer?" Naomi asked Sharkey.

"Yes," Sharkey said. "I could bite her even harder if you want."

"Perfect," Naomi said. "Time to make a decision on who gets to be our sidekicks. Line up!"

The nine remaining kids formed a line, and Sue, Naomi and Tyrone huddled together. Peter was too busy using his purple hat to turn his body into jelly to notice what was going on. And they didn't even bother to ask Jimmy what he thought about the possible sidekicks. He waited to hear their decision.

"Good news for some of you," Naomi finally said.

"And bad news for the rest," Sue said.

Naomi pointed at Slobber. "Congratulations Spit Boy. You're my sidekick."

Slobber pumped his fist and went and stood by Naomi. "I won't let you down," he said, spit flying from his lips.

"You better not," Naomi said.

Sue was next. "Sharkey," she said. "I like your style. You're my sidekick."

Sharkey grinned and clacked her teeth together in a biting motion. "Thanks," she said. "I look forward to biting the Power Council for you."

Tyrone was last. "I pick Weasel," he said. Weasel was so excited she bolted over to his side. She was so much smaller than Tyrone that they looked pretty funny together, but Jimmy didn't dare laugh at them.

"The rest of you, get outta here and forget everything you saw!" Naomi shouted.

When the kids hesitated, Slobber yelled, "You heard her! Shcram!" He picked up his football and hefted it back as if he was going to throw it at them.

The kids bolted from the warehouse screaming. Slobber laughed.

"We're going to get along just fine," Naomi said to her new sidekick.

Although Jimmy didn't necessarily like Slobber very much, he was still a little jealous. He'd always wanted a sidekick, and now all he could do was watch as Naomi, Sue, and Tyrone got to know their new friends. He was still alone. His only real friend was Peter, and Peter was still a big puddle of jelly oozing across the floor. He went back to working on his device while Naomi and Sue discussed what to do next.

"We stick to the plan," Naomi said. "With our new sidekicks, there's no way we'll lose the next fight."

"Where are we attacking?" Weasel asked. Jimmy turned his ear toward them so he could listen better.

"We have to decide," Sue said. "Somewhere that starts with the letter 'I'."

"But not Italy," Naomi said. "We already did Italy."

Yeah, Axel and his new sidekick beat you in Italy, Jimmy thought. He didn't dare say it out loud.

"Um, how about Indiana," Tyrone suggested. "I have cousins there."

"Close," Naomi said, "but I was thinking somewhere more...exotic."

Naturally, Sharkey was the first to figure it out. "India!" she said. "That's where my parents are from!"

"Yes, India," Naomi agreed. "And I know of the perfect target. The Taj Mahal."

On the inside, Jimmy groaned. He'd seen pictures of the Taj Mahal before. It was a beautiful place, and a holy one too. He didn't want to see it get destroyed, but he wasn't about to challenge Naomi and Sue, especially in front of their new sidekicks.

"When do we leave?" Tyrone asked.

"Soon," Sue said. "Very soon."

12

Decoding the secret code

Tanya was still really nervous. She wanted to smile, she wanted to believe that she'd finally found some real friends, but she didn't want to get her hopes up.

She saw Mike and Freddy whispering behind their hands, and she knew they were talking about her. Samantha seemed nice enough, and Britney kept smiling at her. And of course Nikki and Spencer were being super nice. But she wasn't sure about Mike and Freddy and the other two sidekicks, Chilly and Dexter. They didn't seem to like her. None of them had even tried to talk to her.

"And this is the fire tunnel," Spencer said proudly, waving his hands at the fiery torches on the tunnel walls. He'd been giving her a tour as they made their way toward Weebleville.

"Cool," Tanya said. She was so nervous that it was hard for her to say more than just one word at a time.

Spencer never seemed to stop talking, and he said lots of funny things, which made her want to laugh. But she didn't. She couldn't. Not yet. She knew her laugh was too weird to let out, all high-pitched and like a hyena. If she laughed, the Power Council would get rid of her for sure.

"Welcome to Weebleville," Spencer said when they reached a big door. "Help me open it. This door is really heavy."

Spencer pulled at the door with his arms, which were like toothpicks, but the door didn't budge. Tanya reached over him and grabbed the door and yanked. It popped right open, almost knocking Spencer over. "Oh, sorry!" she said. She waited for him to yell at him, to get angry at her clumsiness. That's what Sue or Naomi would've done.

But he just smiled. "Wow! You're really strong, like the Incredible Hulk! Hulk Smash!"

The side of Tanya's lips turned up and she almost smiled. Almost, but not quite. "Thanks," she said. She'd always been strong. It was the only way she could protect herself from the bullies who wanted to beat her up for being too ugly.

As they walked into the giant cavern, loud music blasted from somewhere on the ceiling. It was dance music, the bass thumping, electronic notes screeching. She felt like dancing, but didn't dare. She knew she'd trip over her own feet and make herself look silly. Then the Power Council would see what an oaf she was and kick her out of the Power City forever.

A blur of white fur whipped past her, rolling faster than a speeding car. "Whoa!" she said, taking a step back. "What the heck was that?"

"A Weeble," Spencer said, taking her hand and pulling her forward. He'd been doing that a lot. Grabbing her hand, her arm, leading her. No one ever touched her. The kids at school always joked that they'd probably get warts if they touched Toady Tanya. But Spencer didn't seem to worry about warts at all. "They're all black and white!" Spencer exclaimed, pulling Tanya away from her thoughts of the mean kids at school.

Tanya remembered the Weeble that had given her the powerchest with her powershirts. It had been neon green colored. And most of the

Weebles she'd seen before the Great Adventure were all different colors, too, like fire engine red, macaroni yellow, and sea green. But Spencer was right: every single Weeble she saw now was either black or white.

"Guys, check it out!" Spencer yelled back to the others, who were just entering Weebleville behind them.

"Strange," Samantha said. "Very strange."

"What do you think it means?" Freddy asked.

"Spence, do you think the sidekicks can come up with a theory?" Nikki asked. Tanya liked how Nikki was always asking Spencer his opinion on things. Naomi and Sue never asked her opinion on anything.

"Sure, Boss-Lady," Spencer said. He, Dexter, and Chilly huddled up, whispering, while Tanya watched the black and white Weebles dance to the music, racing around in circles, doing flips, throwing water balloons at each other. Basically they were just having a whole lot of fun.

Finally, Spencer said, "We think it means something big is about to happen."

"Like what?" Nikki asked.

"Something to do with the Power Giver," Dexter said. "The Power Giver seems to control the Weebles, so anything they do must have something to do with him. So if they're changing colors, to black and white only, it's because he wants them to."

"Or *she*," Chilly reminded them. "We don't know if the Power Giver is a girl or a guy."

"Right," Dexter said.

"Then we should ask the Weebles," Nikki said.

"You mean, you talk to them?" Tanya asked. She couldn't imagine talking to the prickly beaver-tailed creatures spinning around them. It was hard enough talking to other kids.

"Sure," Nikki said. She let out a loud whistle. "Roy! Hey Roy! Are you there somewhere?"

Tanya watched as a small white Weeble emerged from the crowd of dancing creatures, rolling to a stop in front of them. He was wearing a red and black Scottish kilt that hung all the way to the ground.

"Roy?" Nikki said. "Is that you?"

The Weeble ran a little paw over his prickly fur. "Nah, it's your Uncle Bob from Sheboygan," the Weeble said in a strong New York accent.

"I don't have an Uncle Bob," Nikki said. "And I've never been to Sheboygan. I know it's you Roy. The last time we saw you your fur was black. What happened?"

Roy looked down at his own fur. "I painted myself," he said.

"Really?" Freddy asked.

"No, you dolt. Why would I paint myself? It just happened, okay kid? One second I was black, and then I turned white. The other Weebles started changing colors, too, but all of them became either black or white. That's all I know, okay? Can I get back to the party?"

"Are you sure this doesn't have anything to do with the Power Giver?" Spencer asked.

"Who are you, Sherlock Holmes?" Roy said. "I'm not telling you anything until the Power Giver says it's okay. Oh shoot!" Roy stuffed his paw in his mouth, realizing what he'd just said. "Forget I said anything, okay?" With that, he rolled back into the party, dancing like a maniac.

"I knew it," Spencer said. "Just you wait. I think the Power Giver could show up any minute."

Tanya's heart skipped a beat. *The Power Giver!* From the time she found her powershirts, she'd wondered who gave them to her. Meeting him or her would be the best day of her life, she knew it. And maybe the Power Giver would also be able to help make her beautiful!

"I like it best when you smile," Nikki said, putting an arm around her.

"Oh! I wasn't…I didn't mean to…I wasn't trying to…" The smile faded from Tanya's lips. She didn't even know it was there.

"Don't worry, I won't tell anyone," Nikki said. "It'll be our little secret."

Tanya really liked Nikki. She couldn't believe she'd ever helped those mean Power Outlaws fight against her. "Thanks," she said.

"Want to dance?" Nikki asked.

Tanya froze. The music was so good and the Weebles were having so much fun... *Yes!* she wanted to scream. *I'll dance.* Instead she just said, "No, thanks. I'll watch."

Tanya started to head for the wall to sit down, but then someone grabbed both of her arms. She whirled around to find Nikki pulling one arm and Spencer the other. "Dance machine! Disco fever!" Spencer said.

Tanya's whole body went stiff as they dragged her out amongst the Weebles. She couldn't dance. They'd laugh at her when they saw what a bad dancer she was. They'd laugh and point and call her names and—

She stopped thinking terrible things and started watching the others. Chilly was dancing like a zombie, her arms outstretched and walking in place. She looked ridiculous, but really really funny. Dexter was shaking his booty and moving his short, stubby arms. It was the silliest move she'd ever seen. The rest of the Power Council were equally funny. Freddy had turned into a turtle and was spinning on his shell while Mike was made of rubber and bouncing up and down on his butt. Samantha had done her little trick where she grew four extra arms and she was waving them all over her head to the music. Tanya watched as Spencer leapt on Nikki's back and she took off, flying above them all, doing loops and spins and ducks and dives.

And they were all laughing at each other. And with each other. They didn't care what anyone thought, so long as they were having fun.

Soon Tanya couldn't help herself any longer. She started to loosen up and her hips began to move. Then her feet, tapping to the rhythm. She swung her arms and bobbed her head and before she knew it she was dancing like a maniac with the rest of them. A couple of times she tripped, but one of the other kids always caught her. The Weeble named Roy even danced with her, sliding through her legs and whirling around her back.

That's when she realized she was laughing, too, her hyena-laugh echoing through the cavern, high-pitched and awful. Tanya clamped her hands over her mouth and whirled around, expecting everyone to be pointing and laughing at her. But they weren't. They'd barely even noticed. They were still just having fun.

They were her friends—her real friends. Tanya smiled the biggest smile of her life.

She looked around for Nikki and Spencer, wanting to thank them for bringing her to Weebleville. Nikki was still hovering over the kids and Weebles, dancing in midair, but Spencer wasn't on her back anymore. She scanned the crowd, trying to find him. *There!* He was off to the side, huddled over a piece of paper. He was writing something and his lips were pressed tightly together, as if he was humming a tune.

Tanya made her way to Spencer, almost getting knocked over three times by spinning Weebles. "Hey, Spencer," Tanya said, approaching him. "Watcha doing?"

Spencer was concentrating so hard he didn't seem to hear her. He *was* humming under his breath. She looked over his shoulder and this is what she saw:

Niagara Falls, New York
Venice, Italy
King Tut's Tomb, Egypt
Mount Kilimanjaro, Africa

Tanya realized it was the list of places where the Power Council had fought the Power Outlaws. Spencer was trying to decode the secret code Naomi had come up with!

But he didn't need to. Tanya already knew the code, because she used to be one of the bad guys. "Spencer, I—"

Spencer looked up. "Eureka!" he said. "I've got it!"

The other power kids heard his scream and came running, huddling around him. Spencer began talking rapidly. "I *knew* there was a pattern.

The places the Power Outlaws attacked weren't random at all. They were selected because of their letters. Watch." Spencer underlined one letter in each of the places, like this:

Niagara Falls

Venice, Italy

King Tut's Tomb, Egypt

Mount Kilimanjaro

"But what does it mean?" Freddy asked.

"They're spelling something," Spencer said.

"I could've told you that," Tanya said.

Mike glared at her. "Then why didn't you?"

"I just...forgot," she said. She knew it was a lame excuse.

"Surrrrrre," Mike said.

"No, really," Tanya said, feeling more nervous than ever. She was struggling to explain herself. How could she explain that ever since Nikki brought her back to the Power City that she felt more at home than ever before?

"She's telling the truth," Spencer said. "She was about to give me the answer, but I didn't let her."

Tanya frowned. "Why not?"

Nikki grinned. "Because he's Spencer and he's weird like that. He probably wanted to figure it out on his own."

"Bingo! Give the girl a stuffed panda bear!" Spencer said.

"So what does the secret message spell?" Samantha asked. "N-I-K-K..." She stopped. "Wait a minute..."

"My name!" Nikki yelped. "The Power Outlaws are spelling my name!"

"Exactly," Spencer said. "But they don't always use the first letter in the name of the place. Sometimes it's the first letter in the second part of the name, or even the third. I'm guessing they did that to make it harder to decode, right?" He looked at Tanya.

She nodded. "It was all Naomi's idea. She thought it would be funny to taunt you with your very own name, Nikki. I'm so sorry we did this." Her stomach felt empty, like she hadn't eaten in hours.

Nikki put her arm around Tanya, and she immediately felt a little better. "It was Naomi and Sue," Nikki said. "I know they're the leaders. But we do need your help with one thing."

"What?" Tanya asked.

"The next place," Spencer said. "We need to know the next target, the one that has an 'I' in it."

Tanya's heart sank. She wished she could help them, that she had the answer. But they hadn't decided that far ahead yet. "I'm sorry," she said. "I don't know."

Freddy, Mike, Chilly, and Dexter frowned at her. Samantha looked away. Nikki and Spencer stared at the piece of paper. Tanya knew she'd let them down.

The music thumped. The Weebles danced. And Tanya felt like running far, far away.

13

To fight or not to fight

"Did you see me? Did you? Was I awesome, or what?" Juniper hadn't stopped talking since they returned to the military base. She was so excited about the battle against Naomi and Tyrone. She was even more excited that they'd won.

The truth was, Juniper *was* awesome during the fight. If not for her heroic climb up the mixed-up clock tower, Axel knew he would've floated away into outer space. Even being King Kong wouldn't have made him strong enough to get back to Earth. Juniper had saved him. "You were amazing, June," Axel admitted. "I would've lost without you." *Worse, I'd probably be dead.*

June grinned from ear to ear, her lips still sticky with gelato from Italy. "I told you I could be your sidekick. Was I right, or was I right?"

"You were right," Axel said. Although it had been a surprisingly good day, Axel was tired. All he wanted to do was take his powerjacket off and go to bed. June, on the other hand, looked like she wanted to run a marathon. She couldn't stop moving around.

"What should we do now?" June asked.

"Go home," Axel said. "Eat dinner. Sleep. You know, normal people stuff."

June frowned. "But we're not *normal people*. We're superheroes. We should be doing superhero stuff."

When Axel was tired and hungry, it made him get mad really quickly. He was getting mad now. "Look, Juniper, I appreciate all your help today, but you got really lucky. We could've just as easily lost. *I'm* the superhero, not you. You're barely a sidekick. Go home."

June's face fell. As happy as she looked a moment ago, now she looked equally sad. "Yeah," she said. "You're right. I got lucky. I'll try not to bother you anymore, Axel *Power*jackets." She rolled her eyes and walked away.

The moment she turned her back on him, Axel's powerbracelet lit up. Someone needed his help. He opened his mouth to call out to June, but the words wouldn't come. He was too tired and hungry. Someone else would have to help them.

During the walk home across the military base, Axel couldn't get June's sad face out of his head. He knew he'd hurt her, but it's not like it was *his* job to make *her* happy. From time to time, his powerbracelet would pulse with bright white light. He wondered who was in trouble, and whether it was the Power Outlaws attacking again.

But he ignored his powerbracelet and kept walking, until he arrived home. His mom was making dinner and it smelled so good. His dad wasn't home yet, but he would be soon. They'd have a nice dinner and then get some rest. Tomorrow he'd think about finding June and apologizing.

After saying hi to his mom, Axel flopped down on the couch and flicked on the TV. He flipped through the channels. Cartoons, some nature show, a celebrity gameshow…nothing caught his interest. A news story popped up and he stopped, his heart beating rapidly in his chest. The headline read: *Taj Mahal under attack by Power Outlaws.*

In the background, people were running and screaming.

On his wrist, his powerbracelet pulsed with white light.

Axel stared at the screen for a moment, remembering June's words to him: *We're superheroes. We should be doing superhero stuff.*

Something caught his attention at the window and he turned his head to look. Two Weebles stared at him through the glass. One was white and the other black. When he blinked, they disappeared, as if he'd imagined them.

He looked back to the TV, lifted the remote, and turned off the news story. He wouldn't be fighting any Power Outlaws tonight.

14

The Taj Mahal, India

"Do you think they might attack somewhere in Indiana?" Freddy suggested. "Indiana starts with the letter 'I'."

Nikki still couldn't believe the Power Outlaws were spelling out her name with the places they were attacking. They'd already spelled N-I-K-K. Next was 'I'. And what would happen after that? Would they spell 'Powergloves' too? That was *a lot* of letters, which meant a lot of places they'd attack, which meant a lot of destruction and people getting hurt. Nikki really didn't want that.

She thought about Freddy's suggestion. She didn't know much about Indiana, but it didn't feel like the right place for an attack. Why not Iowa or Idaho or Illinois? They all started with 'I', but none of them seemed...BIG enough for the Power Outlaws to attack.

Spencer agreed. "I have a feeling the next target will be somewhere really important. I'm sure Indiana is a great place, but it's not famous enough."

Mike said, "How about the Eiffel Tower. That's in Paris, right? And it's really famous, my mom talks about going there all the time."

It sounded good to Nikki. She looked at Spencer to see what he thought. "Sorry, Mike," Spencer said. "It was a good try, but the Eiffel Tower starts with an 'E' not an 'I'."

"Oh," Mike said. "I never knew that."

"It could be an island," Samantha suggested. That sounded like a really good idea to Nikki, but she couldn't think of any really famous islands. Hawaii was famous, but no one really called it Hawaii Island.

"Maybe..." Spencer said.

As it turns out, they didn't need to figure it out on their own, because the alarms blared and the emergency screens descended from the ceiling. At the same time, all of their powerbracelets lit up at once.

"Houston, we have a problem!" Spencer said. The screens showed a picture of the Taj Mahal, in—

"India!" Tanya shouted. She'd been really quiet the whole time they'd been guessing where the Power Outlaws might attack, but now she was on her feet and yelling "India!" over and over again. The screen showed forms in the distance—the Power Outlaws. "We have to stop them!"

Even though some of the other members of the Power Council didn't seem to trust Tanya, Nikki did. She didn't seem like a bad person, just someone who got caught up with the wrong group of kids.

On the screen, people were screaming, running down a straight, narrow path. Beside the path was a long rectangular reflecting pool. Past the pool and the path was what looked like a palace, a beautiful white building with tall columns and a huge ball on top with a long thin spire sticking up in the middle, like a needle. On each side were towers that pointed up to the clouds. *The Taj Mahal!* Nikki thought. None of them realized how close Freddy's guess had been. Indiana sounded almost like India, but they were separated by thousands of miles of land and ocean.

"Huddle," Samantha said, putting her arms around the other kids. With the addition of Tanya to the group, there were so many Power Council members that Samantha couldn't even reach around all of them. Instead, they all put their arms around each other, with their heads in the middle. "We can do this," Samantha said. "We have more kids than them. We just have to protect each other and the innocent people. Good will defeat evil."

Nikki found herself nodding. So were all the other kids. Samantha was a great leader.

"Hands in," Nikki said. All the kids put their hands into the middle, laying them on top of each other. Tanya was the only one who didn't. "Tanya, you too," Nikki said.

Tanya shook her head. "I can stay here if you want. I know I'm not one of you yet."

"Good idea," Mike said quickly. Freddy nodded his agreement.

"No," Nikki said. "She's one of us. She's coming."

"I agree," Samantha said. Britney smiled at Tanya encouragingly.

Slowly, Tanya put her hands in the middle, on top of everyone else's hands. "Power Council on three," Nikki said. "One…two…three!"

"POWER COUNCIL!" all the kids shouted at once, raising their hands in the air.

One by one, they opened their powerchests and put on the power items displayed on their powerbracelets. First Nikki chose a green glove with a drawing of a leaf on it. Then she grabbed a purple one with a muscly arm. She slipped them both on and held Spencer's hand. "You ready?" she asked him. Already the other kids were disappearing, heading for the Taj Mahal.

"Do it, ya Big-Balooga!" Spencer said.

Nikki didn't know what that meant, but she pressed down on her powerbracelet anyway, and the world spun in a dizzying circle. A second later they appeared in front of that beautiful palace she'd seen on the news. People who'd been visiting the Taj Mahal were still running out, trying to get away from the Power Outlaws, who were wreaking havoc everywhere.

There was a massive bull running through the columns trying to poke people with his sharp horns. The bull was wearing a red hat. *Peter*

Powerhats! Nikki realized. Nearby, Naomi was racing by on a skateboard, her pink and black striped skirt fluttering around her. She was pushing people over left and right. Big Tyrone Powerbling was riding an Egyptian chariot and wearing a thick gold bracelet. He tried to run over an old man, but the guy barely managed to dive out of the way. A little past Tyrone was Sue, wearing fluffy purple slippers. She puffed up her cheeks and blew out a big breath. An enormous purple bubble burst from her lips. Sue gave it a push and the bubble shot out, colliding with a woman. The woman ended up *inside* the bubble, trapped. All around Sue other people were stuck in bubbles, too. A few more ladies, a couple of guys, four kids shouting for their parents…there was even a dog!

Nikki was so shocked by the terrible things the Power Outlaws were doing that she didn't even know where to start. Luckily, she had Spencer to help her. "We've got the numbers this time," Spence said, pointing.

Nikki saw that her sidekick was right. Samantha was wearing a brown leather belt and making objects come to life, like bushes and trees. One of the trees stuck out a root and Tyrone's chariot flipped over, crashing into a wall. Freddy had on his fuzzy brown socks and had already created a horde of monkeys. They charged toward Sue, popping her bubbles with their paws and tails. Britney was helping Freddy and his monkeys by using her pink flower-shaped earrings to make soft beds of pretty pink flowers appear beneath the bubbles. When the bubbles popped, the trapped people fell, landing softly on the flower beds. They were able to get up and run to safety. Mike was wearing a scarf with green and red polka dots and had grown an enormous dinosaur tail. He was sweeping it back and forth, forcing Peter the Bull to back away from the people. Even their newest member, Tanya, had jumped into the action. She was wearing a charcoal-colored shirt with a big mouth on it. When she shouted, it was like a physical force, knocking Naomi off her skateboard. She remembered Tanya calling it her Super Shout.

"Hey!" Naomi shouted. "Tanya? You traitor!"

The Power Council was winning, forcing the Power Outlaws back farther and farther, and Nikki hadn't even used any of her powers yet.

"Reinforcements!" Naomi shouted.

What? Nikki thought. The only one who was missing was Jimmy Powerboots. But it wasn't Jimmy who appeared behind them. It was three new kids! One was really big and strong and had drool dribbling out of his mouth. Another was short, but super-fast when she started running. The third had black hair and a big mouth of teeth that she kept opening and closing. Nikki immediately knew what they were: "Sidekicks!" she shouted. Finally, the Power Outlaws had managed to get themselves some sidekicks, and they didn't look very nice.

The girl with the big teeth started biting random people, clamping down on their arms and legs and even one guy's ear. The short fast one was racing through the crowds, grabbing purses and hats and even a few shoes. The drooler was so big he just knocked people over. He even picked up a kid and threw him in the reflecting pool.

Nikki was about to race off to stop the evil sidekicks when Spencer grabbed her arm. "No," he said. "Let us. This is sidekicks versus sidekicks." The other two sidekicks, Chilly and Dexter, were already gathered at his side coming up with a plan.

"What do I do?" Nikki asked. She wanted to help. It was her job as a superhero.

"Find Jimmy," Spencer said.

As usual, Nikki's trusty genius sidekick was right. The last time they'd fought the whole group of Power Outlaws, Jimmy had surprised them all by winning the fight. She needed to locate him, and stop him.

She scanned the crowd, trying to ignore the chaos. That's when she spotted something unusual. An arm was poking out of one of the columns. A leg, too. And a face. *Jimmy's* face!

She raced toward him, but Jimmy saw her coming, and his arm, leg and face disappeared back into the column. Nikki ran around to the other side of the pillar, but Jimmy was already gone. She saw his boots disappear through a wall, almost like a ghost. One of the boots was purple, which Nikki gave him the power to walk through walls. With that power he was going to be really hard to catch!

Not willing to give up, Nikki sprinted under an archway, catching a glimpse of Jimmy as he stepped through another wall. Every time Nikki made it through the entrance to another room, Jimmy was already gone, leading her on a wild goose chase through the Taj Mahal. The only good news was that the place was mostly empty, having cleared out when the Power Outlaws first showed up.

Nikki stopped running, realizing she'd never catch him this way. She needed to be smarter. She needed to think about her powers. Using her green glove she could grow plants at super speed, and her purple glove gave her super strength. In her head, she came up with a plan.

Instead of running, she tiptoed through the next doorway, trying to be as quiet as possible. The room she entered was much bigger than the others, a huge space with incredible arched ceilings and beautiful carved walls. Something about the place made Nikki want to just stop and sit there for a while. It felt like a church.

But she didn't have time to stop and sit because Jimmy was standing at the other side of the room.

"I don't want to hurt you, Nikki," Jimmy said, his voice echoing.

His voice sounded hollow, like an empty old drum. His purple boot was placed next to an orange one that Nikki remembered from one of the first times they fought. Jimmy had almost managed to use that orange boot to pick up Farmer Miller's house and fly away with it! That day, Nikki had won, saving her neighbor by using her super-strength, the same purple glove she was wearing now.

"Then don't," Nikki said. "Stop fighting. Leave the Power Outlaws."

"And join the Power Council?" Jimmy said. "Ha! You guys would never take me after everything I've done."

"Yes we would, Jimmy," Nikki said. "We took Tanya, didn't we?" Nikki took a step forward.

"That's different. She was newer. She hasn't done as many bad things as me."

Nikki took another step forward and said, "If you promise to help us beat the Power Outlaws, you can join us."

Jimmy laughed. "Every time I try to help someone, it blows up in my face." He put his hands together and made an exploding sound, his fingers bursting apart. "There's only one way to end this battle, and I'm almost ready. You could help me with my project, you know. We could still be friends."

Nikki didn't know what he was talking about. *What project?* she wondered to herself. He was up to something big, and all knew was she needed to stop Jimmy before he did anything crazy. "C'mon, Jimmy. Let's talk about this." She stepped forward, getting closer and closer to her arch nemesis.

"Back off!" Jimmy shouted. *Off! Off! Off!* his voice echoed through the big room.

"I can't do that, Jimmy. My friends are depending on me. The whole world is depending on us to keep them safe." She took another big step forward.

Jimmy leapt into action, pointing his arms out to the sides. The walls started shaking and all of the beautiful carvings began breaking apart. A crack formed on one of the pillars as it crumbled under the weight of Jimmy's power. The pillar teetered on its base and then fell. It was going to land on Nikki!

Instinctively, she raised her arms over her head to catch the massive pillar. Most people would be crushed under its weight, but not Nikki. Not when she was wearing her purple super-strength glove. She caught the pillar, holding it over her head. Slowly, slowly, slowly, she walked it up until it settled back into position. It was still cracked and broken, but at least it was upright.

When she whirled around, Jimmy was racing away from her. He passed through the wall and out of sight.

Her heart pounding like a bongo drum, Nikki rushed back through the Taj Mahal, past the beautifully carved walls and sculpted pillars, all the way to the side with the reflecting pool. Her eyes widened when she saw what was happening.

15

The thirteenth power kid

The fight between the Power Council and the Power Outlaws was worse than ever. All the power kids and their sidekicks were fighting, trying to gain an advantage, but neither side would back down. Spencer was shooting his Alien Freeze Ray all over the place, accidentally hitting some innocent people as he tried to freeze the short, fast sidekick who looked a little like a weasel. Freddy's monkeys were running amok, attacking anything that moved. Naomi was racing around on her skateboard, grabbing people and throwing them into Sue's bubbles, which were floating everywhere.

"STOP!" Nikki shouted, at the top of her lungs.

For a moment, everyone froze, even Freddy's monkeys. The superheroes, supervillains, and their sidekicks pulled themselves away from each other, glaring across the space between them.

"You can't stop this fight, Nikki," Jimmy said, stepping through the wall.

Nikki looked at her old enemy. "I can try," she said.

"Jimmy's right," Naomi said. "Only one side can win. Only one of us can be number one in the Power Rankings. That's the way it has to be. That's the way the Power Giver wants it."

Nikki was about to shout back, but then there was a bright flash of light directly between the two groups. She raised her hand to shield her eyes. For a moment she was blind, blinking away spots of light. When her vision returned, she found the other kids blinking and blocking their eyes too.

"Wow," Nikki whispered. A beautiful rainbow had appeared, spreading across the Taj Mahal in a brilliant arc of colors. It came down right between them, where the bright light had first appeared.

"Woohoo! Awesome!" someone yelled from above.

Nikki looked up to find someone *sliding* down the side of the rainbow, using it like a waterslide. *Who is that?* Nikki wondered.

The boy practically flew along the rainbow with his long blond hair streaming behind him until he landed on the ground, skidding to a stop. "So cool!" he shouted.

"Who the heck are you?" Naomi asked, her hands on her hips. She glared at the kid as if he was the most disgusting thing she'd seen all day. The boy was wearing rainbow-colored sunglasses. He was barefoot and shirtless, with deeply tanned skin, and wearing blue swim trunks.

"George," the boy said. "George Powerglasses."

Another power kid! Nikki thought excitedly. All this time she'd thought there were only twelve. But here, standing before her, was the thirteenth.

Naomi stepped forward. "Whose side are *you* on?" she asked rudely.

Sue stepped forward too, her puffy purple slippers swishing on the ground. "Let me handle this," she said.

Naomi frowned at her, but then nodded and stepped back. Sue said, "Hi George, I'm Sue. Let me tell you all the reasons you should join the Power Outlaws, the best and the coolest power kids around." Her voice was icky sweet, like a Popsicle melting in the sun.

Nikki wanted to say something. She couldn't just let Sue convince the new kid, George, to join the Power Outlaws!

But George spoke first. "I'm not on anyone's side," he said.

"What?" Sue said.

"Then why are you here?" Samantha asked, moving to the front of the Power Council.

"To stop the fight."

At that, Naomi laughed. "You? Stop all of us? I hope you brought a big army, because you're going to need it!"

Something about the way George spoke made Nikki wonder about him. There was something he wasn't telling them. "Who sent you?" she asked.

George looked over at her and smiled a bright white smile. "Now you're asking the right questions." Right before Nikki's eyes, his glasses changed from rainbow-colored to iron gray. *How did he do that without a powerchest?* Nikki wondered to herself. The rainbow disappeared from the sky, leaving it blue and empty.

"Wait a minute," Spencer said, joining Samantha at the front. "I *know* you."

"Hi, Spence," George said, tilting his powerglasses down to look at Nikki's sidekick.

"What?" Nikki said. "You *know* him, Spence?"

Spencer nodded excitely, grinning. "I sure do! This is George Kennedy."

Nikki was about to ask her sidekick how he knew the thirteenth power kid and why he'd never thought to mention George before, but Naomi was already speaking. "If George Powerglasses is friends with the enemy, then he's the enemy too!"

The rest of the Power Outlaws shouted "Yeah!"

"Please," George said. "Stop the fighting."

"Not a chance," Naomi said. "Power Outlaws...CHARGE!"

It all seemed to happen in slow motion. Both sides raced toward each other. Naomi rode her skateboard, Tyrone rocketed forward on his Egyptian chariot, Sue started blowing big purple bubbles, Peter the Bull charged. Their sidekicks moved too, the weasel-girl and the biter and the drooler. Even Jimmy rushed into the fight, using his powers to pick up a tree and launch it toward Nikki's friends.

But the Power Council was ready. Freddy's monkeys attacked, Tanya opened her mouth for another Super Shout, Mike swung his dinosaur tail, Samantha made the trees come to life, and Britney started making flower beds in case any of her friends fell. Even Spencer aimed his Alien Freeze Ray while Dexter and Chilly readied cans of Sticky Situation Glue.

Nikki's muscles tensed as she prepared to use her super strength to stop the Power Outlaws.

That's when George Powerglasses used the power of his iron gray sunglasses.

A metal wall exploded from the ground, higher and higher and higher, longer and longer and longer, until it was blocking all of the kids. Nikki couldn't see her friends because she was on the same side of the wall as the Power Outlaws. She heard them shouting through the wall, but couldn't understand what they were saying.

George appeared through the wall. Naomi stepped up to him, until they were nose to nose. "Take down the wall," she said.

"This isn't what he wanted," George said.

"I don't care who wants what," Naomi said. "Bring down the wall."

"He didn't want you to fight," George continued. "He wanted you to compete, to see who'd be the best superhero. He wanted you to listen to what the Weebles were telling you."

"Who?" Nikki said. "Who are you talking about?"

"The Power Giver," George said, and then he vanished.

"Grrrr!" Naomi growled. "I really don't like that kid!"

But Nikki ignored her, because she was too busy looking at Jimmy. She could tell he was thinking about the same three words as she was: *The Power Giver.*

"George may have stopped the battle this time," Naomi said. "But there's no way he'll stop us next time. This isn't the end of the fight." With that, she disappeared on a ray of sunlight. The rest of the Power Outlaws followed soon after, Sue and Tyrone and Peter, until only Jimmy and Nikki were left on this side of the wall.

"What does it all mean?" Nikki asked.

"It means we don't know anything," Jimmy said.

"You can still join the Power Council," Nikki said. "If you want."

Jimmy looked at her, and she could tell he was really thinking about it. "It's not that easy. Even if I wanted to leave, the Power Outlaws will never let me go. I have another plan." Jimmy looked really sad, and Nikki felt bad for him again. She wished he wasn't so confused about everything.

"What are you going to do?" she asked.

"You'll find out soon enough," Jimmy said, and stepped into the wall.

Nikki was alone for a moment, and then the big metal wall disappeared. Her friends rushed forward, crowding around her to make sure she was okay.

"I'm fine," she said. "But we've got a lot to talk about."

That's when she noticed the hundreds of black and white Weebles spread out in a circle around them and the Taj Mahal.

16

Jimmy's super-secret project

Jimmy was smiling for the first time in a long time. His device was finally finished and it was perfect.

His creation was small, about the size of a hockey puck. It was shaped like a waffle, a square with indentations on every side. But packed inside was some serious technology that he'd invented using the power of his red/blue/yellow boots. His device could change *everything*.

He wanted to celebrate with someone, but the rest of the Power Outlaws were too busy planning their next attack. Well, except for Peter, who was wearing his "strong man" hat, the neon green one. Peter had used his hat to grow into a bodybuilder and was standing in front of a mirror and flexing his enormous muscles.

"We stick to the plan," Naomi said. "*My* plan."

Surprise, surprise. Sue was arguing with Naomi. Again. "You had your chance, and your plan isn't working. It's my turn to be the leader," Sue said.

"You'll have to go through me first," Naomi said, already beginning to use her orange skirt to power up her laser eyes.

"With pleasure," Sue said, not backing down. She pointed down at the brown moccasins she was wearing. "You can't handle these." A long yew bow appeared in her hands, along with a satchel of arrows. The tip of each arrow glistened with something wet that Jimmy suspected might be poison.

In a way, Jimmy *hoped* Sue would shoot Naomi with a poison arrow. And maybe at the same time Naomi could shoot Sue with a laser! Yeah! Then they'd both stay out of his way when he did what he knew he needed to do.

Naomi's sidekick, Slobber, stepped up next to her. "You have to go through me firsht," he slobbered.

"I could bite my way right through you," Sharkey, Sue's sidekick, said. She clacked her teeth together a few times.

Oh boy, Jimmy thought, *now even the sidekicks are fighting. Get me out of this place!*

"Hold on, hold on, hold on!" Tyrone said, stepping between the two angry girls and their sidekicks. "Fighting each other won't help us win."

"Yeah," Weasel said, standing next to Tyrone. She was about half his size but somehow still managed to look tough.

Naomi glared at Tyrone. Sue glared at Tyrone. Slobber glared at Weasel. Sharkey glared at Weasel. Jimmy had to cover his mouth not to laugh. He had to admit, Tyrone and Weasel were pretty brave to step between those four kids.

Boldly, Tyrone continued. "How about a compromise?"

"What?" Naomi and Sue both said at the same time.

Weasel explained. "You know, when two people agree on a plan that makes them both happy. My parents do it ALL the time. They like to tell people it's the only way they've been able to stay married for nineteen years."

"What kind of a compromise?" Naomi asked, hands on hips.

"We stick with the plan for the 'P' in 'NIKKI POWERGLOVES.'" Sue opened her mouth to talk, but Tyrone interrupted her. "*Then* we stop with Naomi's plan and come up with a new plan. Together."

"So this will be Naomi's last chance?" Sue asked.

Tyrone nodded his big head.

Naomi chewed her lip.

Sue played with a lock of hair.

"Fine," Naomi and Sue said at the same time.

"Good," Tyrone said. "Now everyone cool off and let's prepare for the big attack."

Jimmy was impressed. Tyrone sounded like more of a leader than Naomi or Sue ever did. He wished they would disappear and then Tyrone could be their leader. Maybe then he wouldn't have to use his device.

The only thing that worried Jimmy about using his device was that George Powerglasses dude. He seemed really powerful. The wall he created was HUGE! For a moment, Jimmy thought about waiting to use his device until he saw whether George Powerglasses showed up.

Then he shook his head and stuffed the device in his pocket.

No matter what, I AM going to use this device, he thought to himself.

17

Tanya's GINORMOUS idea

Nikki and her friends were back in the Power City, and all the black and white Weebles had safely returned to Weebleville. Everyone was talking at once. Some were talking about the thirteenth power kid, George Powerglasses, others were discussing the battle with the Power Outlaws, and the sidekicks were trying to figure out why the black and white Weebles kept showing up everywhere.

No one was listening to each other.

The only ones not talking were Nikki and Samantha, who made eye contact across the room. Nikki nodded to Samantha and they both held up their arms. One by one, the other kids noticed them with their hands up and stopped talking, raising their own hands in the air. It was the signal for quiet. Soon there was complete silence, except for Spencer, who had his finger to his lips and was saying "Shhhhhh!"

"One at a time," Samantha said, and even Spencer went quiet.

Nikki said, "Spencer first. How do you know George...er...Powerglasses?"

Spencer stood on the table so everyone could see and hear him. He loved being in the spotlight. "His real name is George Kennedy. I met him in New York City a couple of years ago when I was visiting my dad. George lives in California, but he was in New York with his dad for some technology conference. His dad is a bigshot at Google, and was part of the design team that created Google Glasses."

"Whoa!" Dexter explained. "So cool!" Everyone was nodding. It was pretty cool, Nikki had to admit.

"But you didn't know he was a power kid?" Mike asked, squinting.

"Of course not," Spencer said. "If I had known, I'd have told you all right away, Lickety-Split!"

Nikki knew her best friend well enough to know he was telling the truth. "But how do his Google Glasses give him all those powers, like the rainbow and the flash bang and the giant metal wall?" Nikki asked. "Normal Google Glasses can't do that, can they?" Nikki honestly didn't know, she'd never used Google Glasses before.

"Nope," Spencer said. "Google makes some awesome glasses, but not *that* awesome! Did you see how he changed his powers without a powerchest? Only the Power Giver could make the glasses give George all those powers. Just like us."

Samantha raised her hand to speak. "Nikki, what happened after the wall went up and we were trapped on the other side?"

Nikki told her story about George. She tried to remember exactly what he said, especially the part about the Power Giver.

When she finished, Britney said, "Do you think he was telling the truth about the Power Giver?" It was the first time she'd spoken, and her pretty green eyes were wide with excitement.

Nikki thought about it. George seemed like a good guy who just wanted to stop the fighting. He had no reason to lie. "Yes," she said.

"That means he *knows* the Power Giver," Chilly said, waving her magic wand around.

"I wonder if George could give the Power Giver a message for us," Mike said.

"We don't even know how to get a message to George," Samantha pointed out.

Those were all interesting topics, but Nikki was more interested in something else George had said. "What George said explains the Great Adventure and the Power Rankings, right? If the Power Giver wants us to compete so he can judge our powers, he's given us safe ways to do it. All these extra fights are not what he really wants for us."

Samantha nodded. "I think you're right, Nikki. But we don't have much of a choice. If the Power Outlaws attack again, we can't just let them destroy everything."

Nikki knew her friend was right. But then how could they end the war with the Power Outlaws? "They're never going to stop," Nikki said. "Even Jimmy said that before he left. Naomi is going to keep attacking until everything is destroyed."

"Then we only have one choice," Samantha said. "We have to capture the Power Outlaws and hide their powerchests."

It was a good idea, something Nikki had tried before. Once she'd stolen Jimmy's powerchest and hidden it away. Unfortunately, Peter Powerhats had the ability to find lost powerchests and he helped Jimmy get it back. That seemed like such a long time ago, even though it was only at the beginning of the summer. "If we can get Peter's powerchest that might work," Nikki said. "But we don't even know where they're going to attack next."

A nervous voice rose up from the corner, where Tanya was sitting by herself. "I might be able to help with that," she said.

Mike stood up. "You said you didn't know where the Power Outlaws would attack next," he said. "Were you lying?" He seemed so angry at Tanya that Nikki felt the urge to step in front of him and tell him to cool off.

"No!" Tanya said. "I swear I was telling the truth. When I joined the Power Council the Power Outlaws hadn't decided where to attack for the 'I' in 'NIKKI.' But they'd already decided on where to attack for the 'P' in 'POWERGLOVES.'"

Mike started to say something, but Samantha cut him off. "Mike, let her talk. She's on the Power Council whether you like it or not. We voted her in and she really helped us in the last battle. So stop being mean."

Mike crossed his arms, not looking too happy about things, but he kept his mouth shut. Freddy moved next to him and patted him on the back.

Tanya opened her mouth and took a deep breath. She looked at Nikki and Nikki nodded for her to continue. "The 'P' was the one letter that everyone was able to agree on," Tanya said. "It was the one place they knew would hurt the Power Council the most."

Something clicked in Nikki's brain and she knew the answer. "The Power City," she said at the same time as Spencer.

Spencer raised an eyebrow and laughed. "You might be a genius after all, Nikks," he said.

Normally Nikki would've laughed along with her friend. But she couldn't, not when the truth was the scariest thing she'd ever heard. "They're coming here to attack us," she said.

"Yes." Tanya nodded. "Naomi and Sue agreed to attack at midnight. The Power Outlaws want to destroy everything you've built."

"They can't do that!" Freddy said, his voice rising.

"They can and they will, Freddy," Samantha said. "Unless we stop them."

"But how?" Britney asked. Her face had turned as pale as a ghost. "Even with Tanya on our side, we almost lost at the Taj Mahal. The Power Outlaws are getting stronger and stronger, especially with all their sidekicks."

"Yeah," Mike said. "If not for that George Powerglasses guy, they've might've beaten us."

As usual, Samantha was the voice of reason in the group. "Maybe," she said. "But we were still fighting. We'll always keep fighting together. That's why we're the Power Council. We fight when others would give up. But we have to fight smarter. Now that we know they're attacking us in the Power City, we need to have a plan. Does anyone have any ideas?"

Nikki immediately looked toward the sidekicks because they were usually the ones with the most ideas. That's when Tanya spoke up, surprising them all.

"I have an idea," she said.

Mike said, "Really? What idea? Surrender?" Freddy laughed, and Nikki noticed that Chilly and Dexter were trying hard not to laugh too. They really didn't like Tanya, even after she'd fought alongside them at the Taj Mahal. It made Nikki sad.

Tanya blinked twice quickly, and for a moment Nikki thought the girl might back off and sit down. Instead, Tanya took a big step forward. "No," she said. "I think we should break the most important rule of Weebleville." Nikki's eyes grew big as she waited for Tanya to continue. "Let's feed the Weebles after midnight. All of them."

There was complete silence for a few seconds, and then Spencer said, "Now that's one GINORMOUS idea!" He was grinning from ear to ear.

18

Hero wanted

Axel was rolling around when Juniper caught up to him. "Hey you!" she shouted.

He didn't answer, because he couldn't. He was wearing his dark orange fleece jacket. Which allowed him to turn into a giant orange. He could've changed back into a boy to answer her, but instead he just kept rolling down the empty backroad.

Juniper was riding a skateboard and doing her best to keep up with him. He had to admit, she was a *really* good skateboarder. He was quickly learning that June was good at a lot of things. But he tried not to think about that. He also tried not to think about how he was starting to think of her as a friend.

Axel didn't have any friends. Axel didn't want any friends. Friends meant he would one day have to say goodbye, and he was tired of saying goodbye.

All he wanted was to be a loner.

But Juniper seemed to have a different idea. "I don't want to be your friend," June said, cutting her skateboard across the front of his path. Axel the Giant Orange was forced to slam to a stop.

He started to shrink, until he was just a medium-sized orange the size of a basketball. Legs sprouted from the bottom and arms from the side. The orange grew a nose, eyes, ears, and then lips. The orange color faded to Axel's normal pale cheeks. "You don't?" Axel said.

"No," June said. "I want to be your sidekick. I want to help people." Axel could see the determination in her eyes as she stepped on the end of her skateboard and flipped it up into her hand. "If I can't be a superhero, I want to *help* a superhero."

"I'm not a superhero," Axel said.

June looked him right in the eyes, and Axel couldn't help but to stare back at her. "The fact that you would say that is exactly what makes you the best kind of superhero," she said.

Axel wasn't sure he knew what that meant, but it sounded smart. A lot of things June said sounded smart. *She* should've been the one with superpowers. She would do great things with them instead of just rolling down an empty road as a Giant Orange.

"I don't know what you want me to do," Axel said.

Juniper smiled and it made Axel want to smile back. "I want you to believe in yourself the same way I believe in you."

Axel thought about it. He had the urge to say one of the usual things he'd say in a situation like this, things like *Leave me alone* or *Get lost* or *Scram, kid!* But he didn't say any of those things. To his surprise, he found himself nodding in agreement. "I can try to do that," he said.

"Thank you," June said.

"And...I'm sorry," Axel said. "For before. I wasn't very nice to you, when you've always been nice to me."

"It's no big deal," June said, but Axel was already shaking his head.

"It *is* a big deal. You saved my life. You are my sidekick. And you are..." The words were stuck in his throat. He swallowed and took a deep breath. "My friend," he said. "You're my friend. No matter what happens."

June grinned. "I always knew you were a big softy on the inside, even if you looked all prickly on the outside. Now let's get ready for battle. The Power Outlaws won't wait long before they attack again!"

Axel opened his powerchest just as his powerbracelet lit up with a bright flash. *It's time*, Axel thought. *And this time I'm going to fight.*

A second later, a single word popped into Axel's head and he remembered something:

Gold.

19

The Power City

It was midnight. The Power Council was as ready as it was ever going to be. All of the power kids had selected their power items from their powerchests. They were spread out across the Power City, hiding in various tunnels and caves, waiting for the Power Outlaws to arrive.

Nikki and Spencer were on the front lines, standing next to the giant net that would catch each of the Power Outlaws when they flew out of the slide that would bring them from Phantom's Peak.

"But how are they going to get past the secret door?" Nikki asked.

"They'll probably just use their powers to bust it open," Spencer said.

Nikki knew her sidekick was right. The Power Outlaws loved breaking things, so why wouldn't they just break down the door? It made her sad thinking how the beautiful Power City was about to become part of the biggest battle the Power Council had ever fought against the Power Outlaws.

"No matter what happens," Nikki said, "you're my best friend and sidekick."

Spencer gave her a hug and a toothy smile. "You, too, Mushy-Musherson."

Nikki laughed and took a deep breath. She needed to focus on using her powers to win the fight. When she was thinking about which powers to use, she considered invisibility but decided against it. She wanted Naomi and Sue to be able to see her when she beat them. In the end, Nikki chose one brown glove and one gold glove. Spencer had agreed.

Now, while waiting, she tugged on the tips of her gloves nervously. The waiting was the hardest part.

But they didn't have to wait long. High above them, the alarms flashed and the speakers blared out a warning: *"Intruders! Intruders! The Power City has been breached. Prepare for imminent attack!"*

Nikki felt the urge to take off and run, pulling Spencer with her. But she didn't. She had a duty to use her superpowers to fight the supervillains. She had to stick to the plan.

Her eyes widened when the first Power Outlaw dropped from the ceiling, because the lights started flashing, spraying sparks of electricity all over the place. It was Naomi wearing a black skirt with a picture of a lightbulb, her dark hair whipping around her face. Lightning crackled between her fingertips as she landed in the net. She rolled over and looked at Nikki, her eyes dark and determined. "Time for some fun," she said, and shot a bolt of electricity at them.

Nikki didn't think, she just acted on instinct alone. Time stopped. Naomi was frozen, yellow lightning streaking from her fingertips. Spencer was frozen, too. He'd managed to raise his Alien Freeze Ray, but hadn't yet pulled the trigger.

Nikki had an idea.

Keeping time stopped, she clambered onto the net and climbed down to where Naomi lay, still frozen. Pulling and pushing and grunting and groaning, Nikki moved Naomi's body into a different position, onto her back with her lightning fingers pointing toward the ceiling, where the slide ended. Then she climbed back down to the floor and studied her handiwork.

"Perfect," she said to herself, snapping her fingers to start time moving forward again.

Everything seemed to happen really fast. First Naomi's sidekick, Slobber, fell from the chute, landing next to her. Then another Power Outlaw dropped from the ceiling. It was Peter Powerhats. Peter was wearing a brown hat, and he'd already tucked his legs under his arms. "Cannonball!" he shouted. That's when Naomi's bolt of electricity hit him in the butt.

His arms and legs jolted straight out and his body went rigid. Steam was rising from his hat. He hit the net with a loud *Twang!* and transformed into a very large porcupine. His sharp quills were sticking in every direction, poking through the netting.

The power of his brown hat, Nikki realized. *Porcupine power.*

Naomi was so confused at what had happened that she kept shooting electricity all over the place. Spencer pushed Nikki to the ground just as a bolt shot over their heads. "Thanks Spence!" she said, grabbing his hand and pulling him back up.

"Run!" Spencer said, yanking her forward just as more Power Outlaws burst from the end of the slide. Before they left the cave, Nikki glanced back to see who had arrived.

Sue was first, her blond hair floating around her. She was wearing knitted gray-and-white-striped slippers. Something about her looked different. Tiny golden wings stuck out from her head. She was clothed in a long white dress tied around her waist with a golden rope. She looked like a Greek goddess from a myth. One of Naomi's lightning bolts shot toward Sue, but she simply raised a hand to block it. The electricity bounced off her palm and crashed into the wall. Just behind her was her new sidekick, Sharkey, the girl who liked to bite anything or anyone in sight.

Next was Tyrone Powerbling, his gold chain bracelets clinking together as he fell from the end of the slide. Nikki wasn't sure what powers those bracelets would give him, but she didn't want to stick around to find out. Following Tyrone was his sidekick, the short fast girl named Weasel.

Last was Jimmy, who was wearing one red rocket boot, and one gold-and-black-checkered boot. Flames burst from his rocket boot and he gently lowered himself to the ground. There was something different about him. He looked more confident, something that had been missing in him ever since Naomi showed up.

Nikki ran, not because she was scared, but because that was the plan. She and Spencer were going to lead them through the traps they'd set up throughout the Power City.

"Get them!" she heard Naomi shout from behind her. Footsteps pounded the floor as the Power Outlaws gave chase.

Sue appeared next to her, running with the speed of a Greek goddess. "Miss me?" she said, and then gave Spencer a big push. It was as if her sidekick had been hit by a train. He flew through the air, heading right for the wall.

Nikki blinked and everything froze, even Sue. Her arms were still out in a pushing motion and she had a big smile on her face.

The first thing Nikki did was to pull Sue's lips down, until she was frowning. That made Nikki smile. Then she ran over and grabbed Spencer's body out of the air. He was heavy, but she managed to get him down and drag him forward. His sneakers scraped against the ground as she pulled him toward one of the many tunnels. She wanted to get them as far ahead as possible before starting time again.

But then time started up all on its own. *No!* Nikki thought. *What's happening?*

Realization hit her like a ton of bricks. She remembered what power Jimmy's black-and-gold boot gave him. The power to speed up time! Every time she froze or slowed down time, he would just speed it up to normal again. Or maybe even faster.

Spencer seemed to understand, too, as his body came back to life. "It's okay, Nikks, you still have your brown glove. And you have me. We can do this!"

They took off, side by side, racing through the first tunnel, which was completely white. The walls, ceiling and floor were so powdery that soon they were covered in white dust. Nikki coughed as they ran. "I hate the chalk tunnel," she said.

Spencer coughed too, and said, "Which means the Power Outlaws will hate it even more, especially after the trap Dexter set for them!" Nikki knew Dexter and Chilly were in the sidekick laboratory, watching everything on video, waiting for the perfect moment to spring their traps.

They raced from the chalk tunnel and stopped, whirling around to look back. The Power Outlaws were in the tunnel now, too, coughing on the chalk dust.

"Now!" Spencer shouted to Dexter in the control room.

A huge poof of chalk dust burst into the air. It was like a thousand kids had clapped a thousand erasers together. It was so cloudy in the tunnel that Nikki couldn't even see the Power Outlaws anymore. She only knew they were still there because of all the coughing.

"Keep going, Mad-Hatter!" Spencer said.

They took off, passing through the next passageway, which was called the rose tunnel. There were beautiful roses of all colors growing from the walls. They were pink and red and white and even blue. The trap for this tunnel was Spencer's idea. "Don't stop to smell the roses," he warned.

Nikki held her breath until they were out of the tunnel. Once again, they stopped to look back.

Naomi stumbled from the chalk tunnel, looking more like a ghost than a kid. She was covered from head to toe in white chalk dust and was still coughing. Her lips opened and she practically growled at them. "You're going to pay for this, Nikki Powergloves!"

105

The rest of the Power Outlaws crowded behind her. They were all covered in white chalk dust, too, and looked just as angry. Except for Jimmy. He was hanging back, just watching. He didn't have any chalk dust on his clothing or skin. Somehow he'd managed to avoid it.

"Come and get us!" Spencer yelled. "I dare you."

That was all it took to send Naomi charging down the tunnel with all the other Power Outlaws behind her. Except Jimmy, who stayed back to see what would happen.

When she reached the middle of the rose tunnel, Naomi stopped. Slobber crashed into her from behind, then Tyrone, then Weasel, then Peter, then Sue, and finally Sharkey. Sharkey's mouth was open, so she almost accidentally bit Sue in the butt. It was like a bad guy pileup on the Villain Highway. Naomi's nose was twitching and she was sniffing at the air. "So sweet," she murmured. "That smell...it's beautiful..." Then she sneezed. This was no normal sneeze, where your head shakes a little and you feel a little funny and tingly in your nostrils. No, this was a whole-body quaking, brain-numbing, lungs-exploding sneeze. The force of Naomi's sneeze was so powerful she flew backwards, ramming into her friends, who were knocked over like pins at a bowling alley.

But Naomi wasn't the only victim of the sneeze powder that Spencer had created and infused into the scent of the roses. All of the other villains, except for Jimmy Powerboots, who had his shirt over his mouth and nose, began sneezing like crazy. If they tried to hold the sneezes in, it only made the sneezes more forceful, knocking them around the tunnel like popcorn in a movie theater popping machine.

"Yes!" Nikki and Spencer said together. They turned and ran into the next tunnel, leaving the sneezing kids behind them.

Nikki knew the trick to the next passageway, which was called the mirror tunnel. This particular tunnel was Chilly's invention, and had thousands of mirrors facing in all different directions, like a mirror maze in a carnival funhouse. The trick was to take two steps forward, one step to the right, two steps forward, one step to the left, and so on until you made it through the tunnel. One wrong step and you could get confused really quickly.

Single file, Spencer and Nikki followed the correct pattern. Nikki giggled a few times because their faces were all over the tunnel, reflected on the mirrors on the walls, floor, and ceiling. Once Spencer's face looked so big it could've been a blimp, and another time her face was all shriveled like a raisin. Nikki loved the mirror tunnel, but she didn't think the Power Outlaws would like it too much!

They made it through, and once more turned back to see where the Power Outlaws were. In the tunnel behind them, the mirrors were now reflecting thousands of Power Outlaws. Naomi's face was still smudged with chalk dust, but now there were red wet streaks from sneezing so hard she'd been crying. Nikki felt a little bad about that, but not too bad considering all the awful things Naomi had done lately. The rest of the Power Outlaws were equally bedraggled, their chalky faces wet from crying.

"NIKKI POWERGLOVES!" Naomi's voice boomed through the tunnel, her mouth open wide on the thousands of reflections. She looked really scary, but Nikki didn't run. First she had to see whether they'd make it through the maze. In one single mirror on the ceiling, she noticed Jimmy Powerboots again. He was holding some kind of a square-shaped metal device, spinning it in his hands. Like before, he looked perfectly fine, like he'd completely avoided the first two traps. And he was smiling.

Nikki closed her eyes and opened them again, and Jimmy's face was gone, replaced by yet another reflection of Naomi's angry snarl.

"SHOW YOURSELF!" Naomi shouted.

"We're right over here," Nikki called back. "Just walk straight ahead and you'll find us." Spencer laughed and she couldn't help but to giggle too.

"You first, Peter," Naomi said.

"Sure, boss," Peter said. In the mirrors, Nikki saw the prickly porcupine version of Peter Powerhats step forward. He kept walking

107

and there was a loud crash and the sound of glass shattering. "Owwww!" Porcupine Peter roared.

"Let me," Sue said, stepping into the tunnel. Nikki's breath caught in her chest as she realized Greek-Goddess Sue would have no trouble figuring out the path through the maze. "Everyone, hold each other's hands," Sue said. "Form a human chain. I'll get you through. Trust me."

"We gotta go!" Spencer said. Nikki nodded and they took off, hoping they had enough time to get away from the Power Outlaws and continue with their plan.

Behind them, Sue called, "We're comingggggg!"

20

Get ready, get set…

Holding Spencer's hand, Nikki dashed into the purple couch room. Mike and Tanya were already waiting, standing on opposite sides of the room from each other.

"They're coming," Nikki said breathlessly, panting from the sprint through the final tunnels.

"The traps slowed them down," Spencer said, "but now they're really angry."

"I'll hold them off," Mike said. "As long as *she* doesn't screw things up." He glared across the room at Tanya, who was staring at her feet. Mike was wearing his brown-and-black checkered scarf with the big minus sign on it. Nikki knew he could use it to decrease other kids' powers, like the Power Outlaws.

This isn't the plan! Nikki thought to herself. "Mike," she said. "You're supposed to use your plus scarf to boost Tanya's power, not your minus scarf."

"I'm not helping *her,*" Mike said. "She'll probably attack me right after I boost her powers!"

"No I won't!" Tanya said. She was wearing her black t-shirt with a picture of a skeleton on it.

"She won't," Nikki agreed. "She's one of us."

"Yeah, and she used to be a Power Outlaw. How do I know she won't switch back?" Mike crossed his skinny arms over his chest.

"Because I'm telling you she won't," Nikki said. "If you can't trust her, at least trust me."

Mike scowled at Nikki, but then uncrossed his arms and nodded. "Fine, but don't say I didn't warn you." He pulled out his powerchest and switched his scarf to the multi-colored checkered one with the big plus sign on it. Now he'd be able to boost Tanya's power.

"Thank you," Tanya said to Mike, but he refused to look at her.

"Good luck," Nikki said. "We've got to go get ready with the others."

"Be safe," Mike said, slapping them both on the backs.

"We'll catch up to you soon," Tanya said.

Nikki nodded and left the purple couch room with Spencer in tow. They didn't know how long Mike and Tanya would last on their own, so they ran the whole way to Weebleville, their shadows flickering under the glow of the torchlight in the fire tunnel.

When they arrived in Weebleville, the others were preparing for battle. Britney was fastening on square silver earrings. Each earring had a turquoise stone fixed in the middle. Freddy was already a turtle, practicing his ninja skills with a pair of nunchucks. Samantha, who was wearing a long silver belt, was shouting orders to the Weebles, trying to get them to line up, but the black and white porcupine-beavers were mostly ignoring her. Instead, they were trying to attack a huge pile of food surrounded by a massive silver dome. Every time one of the Weebles rammed into the shield, they bounced back and all the other Weebles laughed, snorting through their noses. Nikki knew Mike had created the pile of food earlier, and Samantha was using her silver belt to create a dome of protection around the bananas, hamburgers, pizza, donuts, cheddar cheese and other delicious items in the heap. Her mouth watered just looking at the food pile, but no, it wasn't for her. It was for the Weebles, when the time was right.

When Samantha and the other members of the Power Council spotted them, they crowded around. "What's happening?" Samantha asked.

Spencer grinned. "The traps worked perfectly," he said. "Except Sue's a Greek goddess and she was able to get them through the mirror maze pretty easily."

Nikki remembered Jimmy's smiling face. "And Jimmy is being really smart," she added. "He made it through without falling for any of the traps."

Samantha frowned. "This is going to be harder than we thought. What about Mike and Tanya."

Nikki sighed. "Mike was being difficult."

"Because of Tanya?" Samantha asked.

"Yeah, but I think they're ready now. Hopefully they can hold the Power Outlaws off for a while, at least until we can get these Weebles under control." Nikki pointed at the horde of oreo-colored Weebles still throwing themselves at Samantha's shield.

Samantha chuckled. "I don't think it's possible to get the Weebles under control!"

Nikki knew her friend was right, but she hoped Tanya's ginormous plan would work anyway. "What else do we need to do to get ready?" Nikki asked.

"Nothing," Samantha said. "All that's left is to wait for the big fight."

Ugh. More waiting. Nikki scanned the crowd of Weebles until she spotted one that looked familiar. "Roy?" she said.

One of the white Weebles separated from the crowd and rolled over to her. "Me want FOOD!" he said. His eyes were all big and crazy-looking. *What was it about food after midnight that made the Weebles go completely nuts?* Nikki wondered to herself.

"You'll get some food really soon," Nikki promised. "But can you help get the rest of the Weebles into a line?"

Roy threw his prickly head back and let out a snorting laugh. "Bwahahahahaha!" He started slapping his furry knees while doing a headstand. "You're funny, Nikki!" He cartwheeled away and went back to attacking the dome with the other Weebles. Nikki could only shake her head.

A minute went by slowly. Then another. Five minutes passed without anything happening. Then ten. *What was taking so long?* Nikki wondered. *There's no way Tanya and Mike could hold off all five Power Outlaws for that long all by themselves!*

Twenty more minutes passed and Nikki started getting really nervous. Then the door to Weebleville creaked open and fiery light spilled into the cavern.

Eight black shadows walked through the door. "Showtime," Naomi said.

All five Power Outlaws and their three sidekicks stepped into the light. Seven of them were a mess, covered in chalk dust, their faces red, their skin scratched and bruised. Only Jimmy looked unhurt. He was still playing with the metal thing in his hands.

Naomi was holding a beam of electricity in one hand, dragging it behind her. As Naomi pulled the electricity forward, Nikki realized it was a rope, pulsing with energy. And at the end of the rope was a cage made completely from electricity. In the middle of the cage were Mike and Tanya and a whole bunch of skeletons.

"Hi guys," Mike said. To Nikki's surprise, he was grinning.

"Mike?" Samantha said. "Are you two okay?"

Mike kept on grinning. "We're great," Mike said. "Tanya was AMAZING. Her skeletons fought like warriors. She almost beat the Power Outlaws singlehandedly!"

Nikki's jaw dropped. She couldn't believe Mike was saying such nice things about Tanya.

Tanya smiled awkwardly. She looked embarrassed at all of Mike's praise. "Well, I couldn't have done it without Mike's power boost. My skeletons were more like super-skeletons."

Nikki could see exactly what Tanya meant. The skeletons in the cage were bigger than normal people, their bones thicker. They looked really strong. "Great job, guys," Nikki said, wondering how they were going to get them out of Naomi's electrical cage.

"Yeah, yeah, yeah," Naomi said, clapping slowly. "Great job, blah blah blah. They *lost*. That's all that matters. And now the rest of you are going to lose, too, in your own hideout."

Time seemed to stand still for a moment, and Nikki wasn't even using her time-stopping powers. Tyrone cracked his knuckles. Peter stuck his porcupine quills straight up in the air. Goddess Sue clenched her fists. Jimmy kept playing with the weird square thing. A line of drool dribbled from Slobber's mouth. Sharkey chomped her teeth together. Weasel bobbed back and forth from foot to foot. And Naomi raised her hand in the air. "CHARGE!" she yelled, and the fight began.

21

It's a BIG fight

Everything happened so fast that Nikki found herself just reacting without thinking.

First she pushed Spencer out of the way as Porcupine Peter rolled toward him, trying to poke him with his spikes. Next she slowed down time because she realized that Jimmy was using his power to speed it up. She needed time to think. She could feel Jimmy's time-speeding power fighting against her own time-slowing ability. It was a stalemate, so time moved at normal speed. Nikki changed into a lion and leapt away from a bolt of lightning fired by Naomi. Slobber tried to grab her, but she batted him away with a paw. He flew across the cavern and skidded to a stop.

Ninja-Turtle Freddy was going hand to hand with Tyrone, who was trying to grab him. Weasel managed to dive under Freddy's legs and trip him and he fell onto his shell with a loud *crack!*

Samantha blocked an attack by Goddess Sue by creating another shield around her. Sharkey was trying to bite her way through the shield.

It was complete chaos, but Nikki was loving every second! This was who she was, a superhero, fighting supervillains and protecting the world. She let out a huge *ROAR!!!* and leapt on top of Porcupine Peter, using her claws to pluck his sharp quills out. "Ow! Ow! Ow! Ow!" he exclaimed. Soon he was just a round pink little creature. He scurried away, but was too slow. Britney leapt in front of him and used her powers to drop stone blocks in a square around him. More stone blocks appeared, building walls and then a roof. Peter was trapped! Nikki gave Britney a thumbs up and spun around to find the next Power Outlaw to fight.

Nikki spotted Spencer, who was running from Goddess Sue. Apparently she'd gotten bored of fighting Samantha and her protective dome, so Sue had moved on to easier prey. Spencer was trying to shoot his Alien Freeze Ray over his shoulder, but Sue was too quick, dodging the laser beams. She was catching up to him.

Nikki knew it was time for the next part of the plan. "Samantha!" she yelled, and the Power Council leader's head twisted around to look at her. "Do it! Now!"

Samantha nodded and released the giant dome surrounding the pile of food. The Weebles yelled "HOORAY!" and charged the food, diving into the pile with open mouths, swallowing hamburgers and grapes and everything else without even swallowing. "Nom nom nom nom nom!" they said as they ate.

Nothing happened for a few seconds, and Nikki found herself wondering whether something had gone wrong.

But then it happened. The Weebles started growing. Their little round bodies became medium round bodies became big round bodies became GINORMOUS round bodies, until they reached halfway to the high cavern ceiling. "NOM NOM NOM!" they bellowed, still eating.

Nikki couldn't believe her eyes. The Weebles were so huge they were bouncing off of each other and filling Weebleville, squashing houses and street lamps like they were made of paper and twigs.

She glanced at the Power Outlaws. Nikki couldn't wait to see the scared expressions on their faces. But that's not what she saw.

Naomi was smiling, whispering to Tyrone, who was standing on top of Freddy's turtle shell, which was cracked down the middle. Tyrone nodded and raised his meaty hands over his head. "GROW!" he shouted, and that's when Nikki found out the power of his gold chain bracelets.

All around her, the Power Outlaws began growing. Naomi got bigger and bigger, until she was as tall as the giant Weebles. She smashed her hands together and electricity crackled from her fingertips. Peter the Hairless Porcupine grew too, bursting from the stone house Britney had built. His pink body became fatter and rounder and fatter and rounder. Sue went from a normal-sized Greek goddess to an enormous one, her feet the size of cars. Even Tyrone grew and he was bigger than all of them, his head practically hitting the cavern ceiling. The sidekicks weren't left out either. Sharkey's teeth were now so big she looked like a *real* shark and the small girl who used to look like a Weasel was now a towering hulk. Nikki felt a raindrop splash against her cheek and she looked up. *It's not rain*, she realized. Giant Slobber stood over her. Drops of drool were falling from his lips, hitting her like rain. *Gross!* She wiped at her face.

Uh oh, Nikki thought. *We're in big trouble. Literally.*

The giant Power Outlaws charged the giant Weebles, bouncing them around like beach balls, kicking and swatting them across Weebleville. Nikki ducked as a ginormous Weeble flew over her head, smashing buildings along the way.

Everything was completely out of control and Nikki knew they were losing. Mike and Tanya were still trapped in Naomi's electricity cage, Freddy was hiding in his cracked shell, and Britney was building herself a stone house to protect her. Thankfully, Nikki spotted Spencer ducking behind one of the giant Weebles for protection. The only ones left to fight were Nikki and Samantha.

Samantha ran to Nikki the Lion and threw a dome of protection around them just in time. One of Sue's car-sized slippers crashed down on top of them. The dome held up, blocking Sue's kick. Sue laughed a deep "HAHAHAHA!" and kicked another Weeble.

"Look!" Samantha said, pointing toward the food pile, which was almost completely gone. The smallest Weeble Nikki had ever seen was creeping toward the pile, sniffing at the food. Nikki recognized the tiny Weeble right away.

"The Great Weeble," Nikki tried to say, but it came out as a growl.

Samantha seemed to know what she meant and nodded, and together they watched as the Great Weeble picked up a peanut and popped it in his mouth. "Yeehaw!" he screamed, and then started to grow. The smallest Weeble of all grew to be the biggest Weeble of all in a matter of seconds, his head cracking against the ceiling. "YEEHAW!" he shouted again, his voice like thunder.

The giant Great Weeble ran toward the Power Outlaws, his footsteps shaking the ground like an earthquake. First he tackled Peter Porcupine, knocking him back against the wall. Peter sat there, dazed, and began to shrink. Next the Great Weeble made short work of the villain sidekicks by ramming into Slobber, who crashed into Weasel, who smashed into Sharkey. They went down in a heap of tangled arms and legs that were big enough to be tree trunks. Like Peter, they started to shrink.

But it wasn't enough. The other Power Outlaws, Naomi, Tyrone, and Sue, were too quick. They surrounded the Great Weeble and together managed to push him across Weebleville.

It was at that moment that Nikki the Lion knew they were going to lose.

That's when Axel appeared right next to her, his denim jacket loose around his shoulders. Beside him was the dark-haired girl from the video, his new sidekick. "Did you miss me?" he said with his strong English accent.

"About time you showed up," Nikki said, turning back into herself. "We're in a world of trouble."

"Watch and learn, kids," Axel said. He raised his dart gun and fired. The feathered dart flew through the air and stuck into giant Tyrone's knee. Tyrone looked down at his knee, then at Axel, and roared. Then he collapsed, crashing to the ground, and started snoring. "Easy peasy," Axel said. "Next!"

He fired toward Naomi, but she was ready. She shot a massive bolt of electricity at his dart, obliterating it.

"Nice try," Samantha said. "But there's no way you can win with just that little gun."

"Then maybe you should help," Axel said. "And anyway, the darts are just a distraction. June and I have a better plan. Where's Mike?"

Nikki pointed toward the electricity cage.

Axel nodded. "June, you're on!"

"She'll never make it," Samantha said.

"Yes I will," June said. "But only if you guys cover me."

Nikki looked at Samantha, who said, "Okay. Let's do it."

The moment June burst from the protective dome, Naomi and Sue went after her. Axel fired three quick darts, which made Naomi stop to shoot them with her lightning bolts. Nikki leapt from the dome, too, morphing back into a lion, charging right at Sue, who was forced to pull up to fight her. Sue tried to slam her foot onto Nikki's head, but she dove out of the way with lion quickness. The next time, however, she wasn't fast enough. She was about to be squashed into lion jelly! She closed her eyes.

Nothing happened.

When Nikki opened her eyes, Sue's big slipper was being blocked by a silver shield. Nikki looked back at Samantha, who was concentrating. "Thank you!" Nikki yelled and bounded away.

By then, June had managed to reach the cage. She was talking to Mike and Tanya through the electricity bars.

Nikki leapt into Samantha's dome of protection and changed back into herself. "What's she talking to them about?" she asked.

Axel threw her a sly grin. "Remember when you rescued me from the Power Trappers?"

Nikki frowned. "Yeah. So what?"

"Don't you remember how they were blocking our powers?"

Nikki tried hard to remember. Across the cavern, Mike was nodding at June, even smiling a little. Mike pulled out his powerchest and switched his scarf to a gray one with a picture of a hammer on it. Nikki remembered. "They locked you in a *gold* room!"

"Exactly," Axel said. "Only gold can block our powers."

Mike raised his arms and began to use the power of his gray scarf. He could build anything, using any kind of materials. *Even gold.* A wall of gold shot upwards, breaking through the cage, which vanished with an electric sizzle and a whole lot of sparks. Once freed, Mike began building gold panels around the inside of the entire cavern, completely covering the brown rock walls.

When the cavern was plated in gold, it changed everything. The giant Weebles began to shrink, getting smaller and smaller until they were back to normal. The Power Outlaws shrunk, too, all the way down to their usual nine-year-old selves. Naomi tried to shoot electricity at Mike, but nothing happened. Peter was just a kid again, not a hairless porcupine. Sue was still beautiful, but was no longer a Greek goddess.

Samantha's dome of protection disappeared, and Freddy's shell vanished, leaving him just a chubby boy lying on the ground. Britney's stone hut was gone, too. She stood up, her pretty eyes as wide as dinner plates.

Nikki tried to change into a lion, but couldn't. All of their powers had been blocked by Mike's golden walls. And it was all Axel's idea.

"That was…amazing," Nikki said.

Samantha looked stunned. "I…just…thank you," she said to Axel.

"You didn't think I'd show up, did you?" Axel said, smirking.

Truthfully… "No," Nikki and Samantha said together.

Axel chuckled. "You can thank June over there. She convinced me. She's a good sidekick."

Nikki was about to reply, when someone that Nikki had completely forgotten about ran forward.

Jimmy Powerboots. He held up the square-shaped metal device Nikki had noticed before.

"Right now you can't use your powers," Jimmy said. "Soon you'll never be able to use your powers EVER AGAIN!"

22

The powerchest vaporizer

Jimmy placed the device on the floor in front of him. He'd never felt better in his entire life. He was finally going to fix things rather than destroying them.

"What do you think you're doing, you little punk!?" Naomi screamed. "This isn't part of the plan!"

Jimmy wasn't scared of the leader of the Power Outlaws anymore. She couldn't use her powers because of the gold walls Mike had built. And after Jimmy used his device, she'd never be able to use her powers again. "Your plan was never *my* plan," Jimmy said to Sue. "And I have a name, it's Jimmy Sykes."

He noticed Nikki staring at him, her eyes wide with wonder. "I'm sorry I caused all that trouble in Cragglyville," Jimmy said. "I hoped if you saw all the fun we could have with our powers that we'd be friends."

Nikki said, "I never wanted to destroy things, even if I did by mistake a couple of times. I only wanted to help people."

Jimmy nodded. He'd really screwed things up. But it wasn't too late to make them right. "I can fix it," he said.

"Jimmy," Nikki said, taking a step forward.

"Stop right there," Jimmy said.

Nikki stopped. "What is that thing?" she asked, pointing at his secret device.

"Something I used my powers to build," Jimmy said. "It's a powerchest vaporizer."

Nikki's sidekick joined her across from Jimmy. "Vaporizer?" Spencer said. "Wait, you don't mean it will *destroy* all the powerchests, right?"

"No," Jimmy said quickly. "I mean, yes, it will get rid of the powerchests, but only so none of us can hurt anyone or destroy anything anymore. Don't you get it? Kids like us shouldn't have all this power. The Power Trappers were right. We're too dangerous and we have to be stopped before this goes any further."

"Jimmy, no," Nikki said. "This isn't what the Power Giver wants. You heard the 13th power kid, George Powerglasses. He doesn't want us to fight, but he does want us to compete, to practice with our powers and learn to use them the right way."

"There is no Power Giver," Jimmy said. "None of this means anything. Which is why I have to do this. I'm sorry."

Nikki and Naomi both tried to rush toward him, but they were too slow. Jimmy stepped on his device, pressing down a button with his foot. Naomi and Nikki stopped. His device, which was now glowing bright white, started to spin. There was a rush of wind and all of the power kids, from both the Power Council and the Power Outlaws, started shouting at the same time. They were grabbing at the air, as if trying to catch lightning bugs.

No, Jimmy realized, *they're trying to catch their powerchests.*

He felt his own tiny golden powerchest slip from his pocket and rise in the air, levitating over to his device. His device was like a vacuum cleaner, sucking all the powerchests toward it. At the same time, it was blasting air outwards, pushing the power kids back. They were running, trying to catch their powerchests, but the wind was so powerful they weren't moving at all.

Jimmy was at the center of it all, the air whipping around his head like a tornado, spinning the twelve golden powerchests in a circle. Slowly, slowly, slowly…the powerchests grew, until they were full size.

Nikki was yelling something, and Jimmy strained his ear to try to hear what she was saying. "No, Jimmy! Turn it off! Please!" she cried.

For the first time since he came up with the idea, Jimmy was having doubts about his plan. But it was too late for that. Too late for anything. "I can't!" Jimmy shouted back. "Once turned on, the device can't be stopped!"

A brilliant burst of white-gold light shot from the device in all directions, as if the sun and the moon and the stars had all collided. Jimmy could feel the heat on his skin and he backed away one step at a time, holding his hands over his eyes.

BOOM! The whole world seemed to explode, and Jimmy felt himself being thrown backwards. He crunched into the wall, which was no longer gold but rough and stony again.

The light was gone. The wind was gone. His device was gone, too, vaporized by the explosion.

The powerchests were gone. All of them had been vaporized, as if they never existed at all.

And Jimmy smiled a real smile. It was over. No more powers. No more destroying. No more Weebles and Power Outlaws and Power Council and Power Trappers and Power Giver. No more superheroes and no more supervillains. Everything could go back to normal. Finally.

Wait. He sat up.

There. Nikki was reaching into her pocket and pulling something out. It glimmered like gold. She placed it on the ground and opened it. The golden object bulged out and grew bigger and bigger and bigger.

And Nikki pulled a single blue glove out of her powerchest.

23

The Power Team

Nikki took off, flying above Weebleville. Beneath her, all of the other power kids were opening their own powerchests and putting on their scarves and skirts and bling and earrings and jackets and belts and socks and slippers and shirts and hats. They were preparing for battle.

Except for Jimmy. He was sitting against the wall staring at the tiny powerchest in his hand. A tear was running down his cheek.

Nikki felt sad for him because she knew he was finally trying to do what he thought was the right thing. But in her heart she knew the powerchests were not supposed to be destroyed. Yeah, there were bad kids and good kids and they fought a lot, but there was something behind it all. Someone. The Power Giver.

Even though Jimmy's device didn't work the way he'd hoped, it did do one thing: it removed all of the gold from the walls and ceiling. The power kids could use their powers again, and she knew they'd have to fight until someone won.

Of course, Naomi was the first to attack, shooting a bolt of electricity at Nikki. Nikki twisted in the air, avoiding the blast, and dove at the Power Outlaw. Naomi shot a few more lightning bolts, but Nikki dodged them, tackling her. They rolled over and over, coming to rest near Jimmy's feet.

Nikki squirmed away and flew off in time to see the fighting all around her. Slobber had pinned Spencer to the ground and was drooling all over him. "Bleck, yuck, ack!" Spencer cried. Chilly was using her magic wand to pull rabbits out of a hat. The rabbits were charging at Weasel, who was running away from them. Dexter and Sharkey were covered from head to toe in Sticky Situation Glue. Tanya's skeletons were throwing themselves at Sue, who was a Greek goddess again, shoving them away. Porcupine Peter had re-grown his quills, and was using them to poke Ninja-Turtle Freddy inside his shell. Mike, Axel and Samantha were fighting Tyrone, who'd grown into a giant lumberjack, swinging his heavy axe over his head. Black and white Weebles were running and dancing and rolling and jumping all over the place, as if there wasn't a huge war going on.

Nikki knew they needed help, and she finally understood something George Powerglasses had said to them back at the Taj Mahal. *The Power Giver wanted you to listen to what the Weebles were telling you.*

"The Weebles," Nikki whispered to herself. They hadn't been saying anything, but when they changed colors, to black and white, the Weebles were trying to send a message to all the power kids, both villains and heroes. "The yin yang!" Nikki exclaimed loudly.

Her voice was even louder than she thought, echoing throughout the cavern. For a moment, everyone stopped fighting to look at her. Even the Weebles stopped. "What are you talking about?" Naomi said. She pointed a hand at Nikki. It was crackling with electricity.

Nikki took a deep breath and tried to clear her mind. "George told us that the Power Giver wanted us to listen to what the Weebles were telling us."

"That wimp?" Naomi said. "He was just a chicken who ran away when the fighting got too tough for him."

"George didn't run. He chose to leave. There's a difference," Nikki said. "And the Weebles were trying to give us a message when they turned black and white."

"You're nuts," Naomi said. "The Weebles are nuts. You should all run away and join a nut farm."

Nikki ignored Naomi's insults and continued. "The Weebles made themselves look like a *yin yang*, and their message was that we need to *work together* if we're going to find the Power Giver."

"Ha!" Naomi said. "Nice try, but I'm not falling for that. I'll never work with the Power Council, and neither will the rest of the Power Outlaws."

"No," Nikki said, shaking her head. "You're wrong."

Naomi didn't like to be told she was wrong and Nikki could practically see the steam coming out of her ears as her face grew redder and redder. "What did you say to me?" Naomi said.

"You. Are. Wrong," Nikki repeated.

Naomi shouted, "GET THEM!" and shot off a dozen bolts of electricity. Her attack was so quick and so powerful that she was going to hurt everyone in the cavern. Nikki tried to dive out of the way, but the lightning was heading right for her.

"STOP!!!" someone shouted and a mirror appeared from thin air. Naomi's electricity bounced off the mirror and reflected back at her. Her body jolted when the lightning hit her, knocking her back.

"Oww!" she cried. Her long dark hair was sticking straight up in the air and her skirt was singed around the edges. She raised her hands in the air and prepared to fire more electricity.

Nikki's eyes widened when she saw him. George Powerglasses stood in front of Naomi, carrying a mirror-shield. His reflective silver sunglasses covered his eyes. "Just stop, Naomi," he said. She glared at him, but dropped her hands to her sides. She didn't dare to shoot her lightning again because George would just reflect it back at her.

George turned to face Nikki. "You were right," George said. "You figured it out. If you all want to find the Power Giver, then you can't fight anymore. You have to work together. You're all different, but that doesn't mean you can't get along. You have to be like the *yin* and the *yang*, different but part of the same circle."

Nikki understood. "We have to be a team."

George nodded. "Yes."

"A team?" Naomi scoffed. "And let me guess, you'll be our fearless leader?"

"I'm not part of the team," George said. "I'm just here to deliver a message from the Power Giver. But the message is only for those who agree to stop fighting and join together."

"Then you've come to the wrong place," Naomi said. "I think your loser message is for the loser Power Council. The Power Outlaws are leaving. Now." Naomi spun around, finding all the Power Outlaws. "Let's get out of here," she said.

The Power Outlaws just stared at her. "What are you waiting for!?" Naomi shrieked.

"Uh," Tyrone said. "I think I'm staying. I want to hear the Power Giver's message, and I want to be a part of the team. How about you, Weasel?"

"Sure!" Weasel said.

Nikki's heart leapt! Tanya had said she thought Tyrone was an okay guy, and she was right.

"What?" Naomi said. "Fine. Do whatever you want. Be a loser. The rest of us are going."

"Actually," Sue said, putting her arm around Sharkey, "we're staying, too. We know we've done some really bad things, but we feel sorry for what we've done, right Shark?" Sharkey gave Sue a funny look, but then nodded. "Me and my sidekick will join the team if you'll let us, Nikki?"

Sue's voice was so sweet that it was hard to tell whether she was lying, but Nikki couldn't say no. "Of course," she said. "Everyone deserves a second chance." She looked at Tanya, who smiled at her.

Naomi was stomping her feet and punching at the air. "Argh!" she yelled.

Porcupine Peter turned back into normal Peter Powerhats. He scratched his head. "I like teams," he said.

"Then you're in," Samantha said, joining Nikki in the front. "Who else?"

"Me," Freddy said.

"Me," Mike echoed.

"Me!" "Me!" "Me!" "Me!" A chorus of voices rang out. Britney, Chilly, Spencer, and Dexter all wanted to join their team.

"Axel?" Nikki said. "You and June are with us, right?"

Axel tugged at his jacket. He looked really uncomfortable. June whispered something in his ear. "I guess," he said.

"He means 'yes,'" June said, grinning.

"Tanya?" Nikki said. "We really need your help."

"I don't know…" Tanya said. She was looking at her feet and avoiding eye contact with Mike, Freddy, Chilly and Dexter.

"Of course you have to join!" Mike said, putting his arm around her. "Look, Tanya, we were mean jerks before. We thought you were one of the bad guys, but we were wrong."

"We're really sorry," Freddy said.

"Yeah, please join," Dexter said.

"Pretty please," Chilly added.

Tanya smiled a really pretty smile. "Okay. I'll do it. I'll join."

"Yay!" the power kids shouted.

Nikki scanned the cavern. There were only two power kids and one sidekick who hadn't decided yet. Naomi was scowling at everyone, even her sidekick, Slobber, who'd been quiet through the whole discussion.

Then Nikki spotted Jimmy, who was trying to sneak away through the door. "Jimmy?" Nikki said. "Are you with us?"

Jimmy froze. Slowly, he turned to face them. "What? You mean, you'd let me be on the team even after what I tried to do? Even after I tried to vaporize all the powerchests?"

Nikki smiled and nodded. "Yes. We'd love to have you on the team."

Jimmy seemed completely and utterly shocked, his eyes as wide as flying saucers and his mouth open like a fish. "I—I—I—" he stuttered.

"Just say yes," Nikki said.

"Yes," Jimmy said. "I'd really like that." He marched forward and joined the rest of the kids.

"Slobber?" Nikki said. "You don't have to be Naomi's sidekick if you don't want to. A lot of us still need sidekicks."

Slobber looked like he was about to step forward, but Naomi grabbed his arm. "Don't you dare," she growled. "Let's go." There was a flash of bright light and then Naomi and her sidekick were gone.

Nikki turned to Samantha and their eyes met. They both seemed to know what the other was thinking. "You say it," Nikki said.

Samantha nodded. "From this point forward, there is NO Power Council or Power Outlaws! From now on, we're the Power Team!"

Everyone cheered, even the Weebles, who had all magically changed back to their normal colors, blue and peach and orange and brown and everything in between.

24

George's final message

The party went on for a long time. Everyone danced. Everyone smiled. Everyone had fun and seemed happy.

Everyone used their powers, too, but not to fight. Just for fun. Mike rebuilt Weebleville and made it even better, with taller buildings, brighter lights, and louder music. Lots of the kids flew through the cavern, playing follow the leader. Others danced with the Weebles, challenging them to dance-offs like Nikki had a long time ago. The Weebles usually won—they were *really* good dancers, especially Bo Diddy.

George watched everything from a rooftop, smiling to himself behind purple sunglasses.

For a while, Nikki kept an eye on Sue and Sharkey, because she still didn't trust them, but they were just having fun, too. Sharkey didn't even bite a single kid or Weeble, although Nikki caught her gnawing on a fire hydrant.

Maybe we can all just be friends now, Nikki thought to herself, as she flew with Spencer on her back.

"You figured it out, Einstein," Spencer said. "You were much more of a genius than me!"

Nikki turned her head to look at her best friend. "*We* figured it out," she said. "If you didn't explain what the yin yang meant, I'd never have understood." She lifted her hand and Spencer grabbed it, squeezing.

"We make a great team!" Spencer yelled as Nikki swooped to the ground and set him back on his feet.

Once more, they joined the dance party, spinning and moving until their legs were so tired that had to sit down and rest. Nikki and Spencer sat side by side, and soon more and more members of the Power Team began to join them. Once they were all gathered together, one of the Weebles broke off from the rest.

It was Roy. "The Great Weeble told me to tell you that he has a message for you."

"I think we're finally ready for it," Nikki said.

"Good," Roy said. "Here he is now!"

The smallest Weeble of all rolled forward, raising a cloud of dust as he skidded to a stop. "Hey, y'all!" the Great Weeble said. "I gots a real important message for y'all. George wants ta say sumthin'."

Everyone laughed. Roy had a message from the Great Weeble who had a message from George, who wanted to talk to them. It was a funny way of doing things, but somehow it felt exactly right.

Samantha spotted George first. "There!" she pointed. George was riding a beautiful white flying horse with broad purple wings. His Google glasses were purple, too, matching the horse's wings.

"A Pegasus," Spencer said. "Holy chicken wings!"

The magical animal landed softly in front of them. George dismounted and patted his steed on the head. "Good girl," he said. He pulled a carrot from his pocket and the animal ate it from his hand.

George turned toward the Power Team. He took off his purple glasses and the Pegasus disappeared. "There were supposed to be twelve of you," he said.

Naomi, Nikki thought. She wondered whether missing one power kid would screw everything up for the rest of them.

"But," George said, raising a finger in the air. "I just talked to the Power Giver and he decided to continue with the quest anyway."

"Quest?" Spencer said. "What quest?"

"To find the Power Giver," Nikki answered. She knew she was right even before George nodded.

"Yes," George Powerglasses said. "The summer is almost over, and the Power Giver has yet to decide the final Power Rankings. Only one power kid can win the Best and Most Wonderful Prize."

"It's going to be me," Sue said.

George ignored her. "But first you have to work together to find the Power Giver. As you might've noticed, you all have the same birthday. In fact, you were all born at the exact same second in time, which makes you all connected. You'll all turn ten years old in exactly one week. If you can't find the Power Giver by then, no one wins and you'll all go back to being normal kids."

Silence filled the cavern. Even the Weebles had gone quiet. After coming so far and working so hard, the thought of losing their powers was too scary. Nikki stood up. "We'll do it," she said. "We'll find the Power Giver."

Spencer stood up next to her. "We'll do it together," he said.

"Yes," Samantha said, joining them. "We're the Power Team now."

All the other power kids and their sidekicks stood up one by one. "Power Team! Power Team! Power Team!" they chanted as one. Even Sue and Sharkey joined in the cheer.

When they'd quieted once more, George said, "Good, I think you're ready. Get some rest. First thing tomorrow we'll be leaving on the quest."

"Where are we going?" Spencer asked.

George paused for a moment and everyone seemed to lean in closer.

He flashed a big white smile. "To the Power Island!" he yelled.

THE END (of this adventure!)

Meet the 14th and final power kid! Keep reading for a peek into David Estes's sixth and final book in the Nikki Powergloves adventure, *Nikki Powergloves and the Power Giver.*

Are you a teacher or librarian interested in having an author speak in person or via Skype at your school or library? If so, please contact the author at davidestesbooks@gmail.com. The author also welcomes requests from interested parents and their children.

Power Team Card

Hidden Identity: Nikki Powergloves
Birth Name: Nikki Nickerson
Age: 9
Height: 4 feet, 2 inches
Weight: 67 pounds
Sidekick: Spencer Quick, certified genius
Known Allies: Samantha Powerbelts, Freddy Powersocks, Michael Powerscarves, Britney Powerearrings, Tanya Powershirts, Axel Powerjackets
Source of Power: Gloves

Powers

Glove Color	Glove Picture	Power
White	Snowflake	Create ice
Red	Flame	Create fire
Light blue	Bird	Fly
Black & yellow	Lightning Bolt	Control the weather
Green	Leaf	Super-grow plants
Purple	Muscly arm	Super-strength
Orange	Shoes	Super-speed
Gray	No picture	Invisibility
Brown	Paw print	Transform into an animal
Pink	Tarot card	See the future
Gold	Clock	Freeze or slow down time
Peach	Two identical stick figures	Transform into someone else

Power Team Card

Hidden Identity: Samantha Powerbelts
Birth Name: Samantha Jane McKinley
Age: 9
Height: 4 feet, 6 inches
Weight: 77 pounds
Sidekick: Dexter Chan, excellent booby trapper
Known Allies: Nikki Powergloves, Freddy Powersocks, Michael Powerscarves, Britney Powerearrings, Tanya Powershirts, Axel Powerjackets
Source of Power: Belts

Powers

Belt Color	Belt Picture	Power
Brown	Dancing teddy bear	Make objects come to life
Peach	Six-armed girl	Grow extra arms/legs
Multi-colored	Paintbrush	Change objects' color
Silver	Shield	Dome of protection
Gold	Key	Open any door/lock
Bright red	Smile	Make people laugh
White	Gum	Shoot sticky stuff
Blue	Snorkel	Breathe underwater
Orange	Rope	Shoot ropes from hands
Clear	Diamonds	Turn rocks to jewels
Green	Walking trees	Make trees come alive
Yellow	Spider	Climb walls like a spider

Power Team Card

Hidden Identity: Freddy Powersocks
Birth Name: Frederick Nixon
Age: 9
Height: 4 feet, 5 inches
Weight: 95 pounds
Sidekick: Chilly Weathers, amateur magician
Known Allies: Nikki Powergloves, Samantha Powerbelts, Michael Powerscarves, Britney Powerearrings, Tanya Powershirts, Axel Powerjackets
Source of Power: Socks

Powers

Sock Color	Sock Picture	Power
White with black polka dots	Dog barking at a boy	Ability to speak to animals
Gray	Astronaut	Anti-gravity
Camouflage	Chameleon	Camouflage himself
Gold	Wristwatch	Change rate of time
Black	Nunchucks	Ninja skills
Peach	Girl slapping a boy	Distance slap
Pink	Brain	Read people's thoughts
Brown	Shovel	Dig huge tunnels
Black & Yellow	Bumblebee	Turn into a bumblebee
Purple	Microphone	Impersonate voices
Green	Turtle shell	Grow a shell
Fuzzy brown	Monkey	Control a horde of monkeys

Power Team Card

Hidden Identity: Mike Powerscarves
Birth Name: Michael Jones
Age: 9
Height: 4 feet, 2 inches
Weight: 67 pounds
Sidekick: None
Known Allies: Nikki Powergloves, Samantha Powerbelts, Freddy Powersocks, Britney Powerearrings, Tanya Powershirts, Axel Powerjackets
Source of Power: Scarves

Powers

Scarf Color	Scarf Picture	Power
Black	Car tire	Turn body to rubber
Blue/Gold striped	Tall pole	Leap high in the air
Gray	Hammer	Ability to build anything
Green	Ice cream cone	Create food
Brown striped	Tornado	Spin tornado-fast
Red & Yellow polka dots	10 stick figures	Break into 10 mini-Mikes
Black & white	Magnifying glass	Disappear sideways
All colors checkered	Plus sign	Boost other kids' powers
White	Steering wheel	Drive any vehicle
Brown & black checkered	Minus sign	Decrease other kids' powers
Orange	Hovercraft	Ride a hovercraft
Green & red polka dots	Dinosaur tail	Grow dinosaur tail

Power Team Card

Hidden Identity: Britney Powerearrings
Birth Name: Britney Mosely
Age: 9
Height: 4 feet, 2 inches
Weight: 63 pounds
Sidekick: None
Known Allies: Nikki Powergloves, Samantha Powerbelts, Freddy Powersocks, Michael Powerscarves, Tanya Powershirts, Axel Powerjackets
Source of Power: Earrings

Powers

Earring Color	Earring Shape	Power
Silver	Large hoops	Super discs
Red	Hearts	Love potion
Blue	Butterflies	Change into butterfly
Clear	Diamonds	Become as hard as diamonds
Gold	Small hoops	Mini discs
Black	Long dangly	Pixie sticks
Green	Leaves	Leaf monster
Pink	Flowers	Soft flower bed
Brown	Feathers	Pointy feather attack
White	Angel wings	Grow angel wings
Silver with turquoise stone	Square with inlaid gem	Create big stone blocks
Red ruby	Gemstones	Red laser beams

Power Team Card

Hidden Identity: Axel Powerjackets
Birth Name: Axel Grant
Age: 9
Height: 4 feet, 8 inches
Weight: 75 pounds
Sidekick: Juniper (June the Goon) David, hero in training
Known Allies: Nikki Powergloves, Samantha Powerbelts, Freddy Powersocks, Mike Powerscarves, Britney Powerearrings, Tanya Powershirts
Source of Power: Jackets

Powers

Jacket Color	Jacket Picture	Power
Blue denim	Feathered darts	Dart gun
Black leather	Ghost	Ghost attack
Beige cloth	Cow	Cow stampede
Blue windbreaker	Eagle	Sprout wings
Heavy gray wool	Slinky	Slinky movement
Blue & red flannel	Ape wearing a crown	Turn into King Kong
Red nylon	Rocket	Turn into a missile
Green pullover	Elf	Elf mischief
White sweatshirt	Ski poles	Super skier
Dark orange fleece	Orange fruit	Become a giant orange
Brown tattered zip-up	Boot	Big boot
Yellow stylish	Ferrari	Yellow Ferrari driver

Power Team Card

Hidden Identity: Jimmy Powerboots (previously known as Jimmy- Boy Wonder)

Birth Name: Timothy Jonathan Sykes (nicknamed Jimmy)

Age: 9

Height: 4 feet, 1 inch

Weight: 65 pounds

Sidekick: unknown

Known Allies: Peter Powerhats, Sue Powerslippers, Tyrone Powerbling

Source of Power: Boots

Powers

Boot Color	Boot Picture	Power
Black	Cracked ground	Powerstomp
Purple	One leg on each side of a wall	Walk through walls
Orange	Floating bananas	Move objects with mind
Red	Boots with flame	Rocket boots
White	5 identical stick figures	Clone himself
Yellow	Half-boy here, half-boy there	Teleport
Blue	Wall of water	Control water
Brown	Big ear	Super senses
Green	Computer	Computer hacking
Red/blue/yellow	Wires	Skills with electronics
Gray	Yellow pages	Find anyone in the world
Gold & black checkered	Clock	Speed up time

Power Team Card

Hidden Identity: Peter Powerhats
Birth Name: Peter Hurley
Age: 9
Height: 4 feet, 10 inch
Weight: 100 pounds
Sidekick: unknown
Known Allies: Jimmy Powerboots, Sue Powerslippers, Tyrone Powerbling

Source of Power: Hats

Powers

Hat Color	Hat Picture	Power
Bright gold	Powerchest	Find lost powerchests
Neon green	Strong man	Grow big and strong
Black	Cannonball	Turn into cannonball
Gray	Stones	Makes stones form
Red	Bull horns	Transform into a raging bull
Peach	Big hand	Grow big hands
Blue	Big wheels	Drive a monster truck
Orange	Mouth and fire	Burp fireballs
Green	Fingers holding nost	Stinky farts
Purple	Strawberry jelly	Turn body to jelly
Brown	Porcupine	Cover body in prickly spines
Clear	Teardrops	Make people cry

Power Team Card

Hidden Identity: Tyrone Powerbling
Birth Name: Tyrone Mitchell
Age: 9
Height: 5 feet, 2 inches
Weight: 110 pounds
Sidekick: Weasel (real name unknown)
Known Allies: Jimmy Powerboots, Peter Powerhats, Sue Powerslippers, Tanya Powershirts
Source of Power: Bling (jewelry)

Powers

Bling Color	Type of Bling	Power
Gold	Watch	Turn into a Cyclops
Gold	Stud earrings	Become a Greek god
Gold	Chain bracelets	Make things bigger
Gold	Ring	Make things smaller
Gold	Thin necklace	Super-punch!
Gold	Crown	Drop bombs
Gold	Walking stick	Shoot torpedoes
Gold	Belt buckle	Ride a wild mustang
Gold	Chain necklace	Become Paul Bunyan
Gold	Pocket watch	Create black holes
Gold	Sunglasses	Drive a race car
Gold	Thick bracelet	Drive an Egyptian chariot

Power Team Card

Hidden Identity: Sue Powerslippers
Birth Name: Susan Hopper
Age: 9
Height: 4 feet, 0 inches
Weight: 55 pounds
Sidekick: Shakti Shahara, nicknamed "Sharkey"
Known Allies: Jimmy Powerboots, Peter Powerhats, Tyrone Powerbling
Source of Power: Slippers

Powers

Slipper Color	Slipper Design	Power
Green	Lightning bolt shaped	Mind muddler
Pink	Ballet slippers	Light on her feet
Silver	Metal	Robo Sue
White	Feathery	Grow bird wings
Blue & yellow	Shooting stars	Falling star attack
Yellow	Ducks	Quack attack
Brown	Moccasins	Shoot poisoned arrows
Green	Crocodile skin	Turn into a crocodile
Black	Snakeskin	Turn people to stone with her eyes
Blue	Fluffy	Turn into a mermaid
Purple	Poofy	Create big bubbles
Gray and white striped	Knitted	Become a Greek goddess

Power Team Card

Hidden Identity: Tanya Powershirts
Birth Name: Tanya O'Rourke
Age: 9
Height: 4 feet, 6 inches
Weight: 70 pounds
Sidekick: unknown
Known Allies: Tyrone Powerbling, Nikki Powergloves, Samantha Powerbelts, Freddy Powersocks, Mike Powerscarves, Britney Powerearrings, Axel Powerjackets
Source of Power: Shirts

Powers

Shirt Color	Shirt Picture	Power
Gray	Shark's teeth	Become a shark
Black	Skeleton	Skeleton army
White	Guy hanging onto a light pole	Control the wind
Red	Spider	Become a tarantula
Orange	Balloon	Take off like a hot air balloon
Ble	Car	Transform into a car
White & black striped	Mummy	Create mummies
Brown	Weird creature	Become a bog monster
Green	Green splat	Shoot slime balls
Silver	Knight	Suit of armor
Black	Closed eye	Cause temporary blindness
Charcoal	Big mouth	Super-shout!

Outcast Card

Hidden Identity: Naomi Powerskirts
Birth Name: Naomi Lee
Age: 9
Height: 4 feet, 0 inches
Weight: 55 pounds
Sidekick: Dante James, nicknamed "Slobber"
Known Allies: None
Source of Power: Skirts

Powers

Skirt Color	Skirt Picture	Power
Yellow	Sun	Travel on light beams
Green	Ogre	Turn into an ugly monster
Blue	Three skirts	Change powers fast
Black	Light bulb	Control electricity
Brown	Mud	Create gobs of mud
Pink	Gymnast	Gymnastics skills
Purple	Mirror	Mix up the world
Gray	Foot on water	Walk on anything
Orange	Closed eye	Laser winks
Pink & black striped	Skateboard	Skateboarding skills
Black with green polka dots	Plant with arms	Grow fighting plants
Turquoise	Pigeon	Attack pigeons

Power Giver Card

Hidden Identity: George Powerglasses
Birth Name: George Kennedy
Age: 9
Height: 4 feet, 3 ¾ inches
Weight: 77 pounds
Sidekick: None
Known Allies: The Power Giver
Source of Power: Google Glasses

Powers

Lens Color	Lens Symbol	Power
Green	Venus fly trap	Turn people into plants
Purple	Pegasus	Pegasus appears
Red	Ring of fire	Human torch with laser eyes
Blue	Dolphin	Grow fins and flipper
Black	Panther	Transform into panther
Brown	Globe	GPS locator
White	Black outline of person	See invisibility
Reflective silver	Oval mirror	Deflect attacks
Yellow	Sunburst	Flash bang!
Rainbow	Rainbow	Create rainbows
Neon pink	A hand	"Borrow" powers
Iron gray	Wall	Big metal wall
Clear	Raindrops	Giant raindrops

Acknowledgements

Kids are awesome! I write these books for you, thank you so very much for reading about Nikki and her adventures.

The biggest thanks always goes to my wife, Adele, for being SO supportive of my endless list of writing projects. Without you, life's journey wouldn't mean anything.

A HUGE thank you and a leaping high five to my incredible team of kid beta readers and their 3rd grade teacher, Mrs. Clanton. In my opinion, Sue Ann Clanton is deserving of Teacher of the Year. She cares more for her students and their education than anyone I've ever met, and she's created a learning environment that her students will remember for the rest of their lives. Thank you for all that you do, Mrs. Clanton! And thank you to her class of 2015: Braden Routier, Sydnee Thompson, Sheridan Reedy, Rhett Connors, Clancy Adolph, Claire Verhulst, Slate Page, and Riggs Rotenberger! You are amazing beta readers and helped me make this book even better.

I also have to say thank you and give a big virtual hug to one of my Nikki Powergloves super-readers, Katee Hollenbeck. Not only do you have superpowers, but I've heard from a reliable source that you're the best granddaughter EVER.

Lastly, thanks to my cover artist and friend, Tony Wilson at Winkipop Designs, who has helped me bring this series to life from day one!

Discover other books by David Estes available through the author's official website: http://davidestesbooks.blogspot.com or through select online retailers including Amazon.

<u>Children's Books by David Estes</u>

The Nikki Powergloves Adventures:
Nikki Powergloves- A Hero is Born
Nikki Powergloves and the Power Council
Nikki Powergloves and the Power Trappers
Nikki Powergloves and the Great Adventure
Nikki Powergloves vs. the Power Outlaws
Nikki Powergloves and the Power Giver

<u>Young-Adult Books by David Estes</u>

The Dwellers Saga:
Book One—The Moon Dwellers
Book Two—The Star Dwellers
Book Three—The Sun Dwellers
Book Four—The Earth Dwellers

The Country Saga (A Dwellers Saga sister series):
Book One—Fire Country
Book Two—Ice Country
Book Three—Water & Storm Country
Book Four—The Earth Dwellers

Salem's Revenge:
Book One—Brew
Book Two—Boil
Book Three—Burn

The Slip Trilogy:
Book One—Slip
Book Two—Grip
Book Three—Flip

I Am Touch

The Evolution Trilogy:
Book One—Angel Evolution
Book Two—Demon Evolution
Book Three—Archangel Evolution

Connect with David Estes Online

Facebook:
http://www.facebook.com/pages/David-Estes/130852990343920

Author's blog:
http://davidestesbooks.blogspot.com

Smashwords:
http://www.smashwords.com/profile/view/davidestes100

Goodreads author page: http://www.goodreads.com/davidestesbooks

Twitter:
https://twitter.com/#!/davidestesbooks

About the Author

After growing up in Pittsburgh, Pennsylvania, David Estes moved to Sydney, Australia, where he met his wife, Adele. Now they travel the world writing and reading and taking photographs.

1

Power Island! Power Island! Power Island!

Nikki Powergloves couldn't stop smiling. Standing on top of Phantom's Peak with the wind in her hair, she had never felt better. Every time she thought about George Powerglasses's promise to guide her and her friends to the Power Island to find the Power Giver, her lips would automatically curl up on each side.

"What are you grinning about, Clown-Face?" Spencer asked. He opened the secret portal that led into the mountain.

"Your mom," Nikki said, still grinning. Nikki had recently discovered how funny "Your Mom" jokes could be. George Powerglasses knew about a thousand of them.

"Ha ha, very funny," Spencer said. "That was so funny I could only laugh on the inside."

"I was just thinking about—" Nikki started to say.

"The Power Island," Spencer finished. "I can read your mind like a book."

Nikki groaned. She could never keep secrets from her best friend. Spencer was a genius in a lot of ways, including mind reading, and he didn't even need superpowers to do it.

"Helloooooooo!" Spencer shouted into the tunnel. His voice echoed into the distance: *HELLOOOOO! Hellooooo! Helloooooooo!* He turned back to her. "Are you ready to face the Power Giver?"

Nikki shrugged. She wasn't really sure. Over the last two days she'd gone home to see her parents and her dog, Mr. Miyagi. She'd eaten her mom's delicious home-cooked meals, lasagna and roast chicken and stir fry. Before Nikki left to return to the Power City, she hugged her mom and dad harder than she'd ever hugged them.

"What was that for?" her dad had asked, raising an eyebrow.

"Just...just because I love you guys," Nikki had said.

Now she wondered whether she would ever see her parents again. She hoped so, otherwise she would miss them too much.

"Nikki?" Spencer said, waving a hand in front of her face. "Earth to Nikki!"

"Oh...sorry!" Nikki said. "I was just thinking about—"

"Your parents," Spencer finished, once more reading her mind. Above them, the wind howled and the clouds swirled. Each cloud was a different color, like a beautiful rainbow.

Looking back at Spencer, Nikki nodded. "Do you think we'll ever see our parents again?"

"Of course!" Spencer exclaimed. "You're Nikki Powergloves and you've got a genius sidekick. We'll *always* come out on top."

Nikki wasn't so sure, but she appreciated her friend's optimism. She squeezed his hand. "Let's go. The other kids are waiting."

"Me first!" Spencer shouted, diving headfirst into the dark tunnel. He screamed a high-pitched scream and disappeared from sight.

Nikki laughed. Even though she was worried about missing her parents, she was so excited that it felt like a thousand tiny feathers were tickling the inside of her stomach. After all, today was THE DAY. George had asked all the members of the Power Team to return to the

Power City on this particular day, so they could leave for the Power Island together.

Nikki took a deep breath and then jumped into the hole. Soon she was screaming too, sliding down the biggest, twistiest, fastest slide in the whole world. Bright gold, blue, and red lights flashed on and off, illuminating funny pictures. Like a monkey giving a baby a piggyback ride. And a rhinoceros sprouting wings and flying high in the clouds. She giggled and giggled until the slide dropped suddenly, making her stomach fly up into her throat. And then she was free falling, emerging from the dark tunnel into a brightly lit cavern.

When she landed on the net next to Spencer, she bounced three times before coming to a stop. "Awesome," she breathed.

"Fun every time," Spencer agreed. "Do we have time to do it again?"

As much as Nikki wanted to say "yes," they had more important things to do today. "Sorry, Spence, but we're already late."

A giant metal claw was already moving overhead, eventually stopping directly above them. With a lurch, the claw dropped down and picked them up. "Whee!" Spencer yelled, rocking the claw back and forth as it transported them over the net and onto the ground.

Once they were on their feet, they wasted no time. They ran through a large arched doorway, past a bunch of robots and vehicles moving around on their own, and down the first tunnel on the right. This particular tunnel was called the banana tunnel, and as they ran, an enormous yellow banana unpeeled itself on each side. "Smells like a good day," Spencer said, sniffing the air.

The next tunnel was called the wormhole, because hundreds of wriggly, slimy earthworms slid through the dirt walls and ceiling. There were even some worms squirming under Nikki's feet, and she had to do a funny dance to avoid stepping on them. "Ew," she said. "I hate this tunnel." Normally she would avoid going this way, but it was the fastest route to Weebleville, bypassing the purple couch room.

Weebleville was the meeting place for today, and she didn't want to be late.

Spencer grabbed a worm and tried to stick it in Nikki's face, but she used the power of the orange glove she was wearing to race away from him at super speed. "No fair, Speedy-Gonzalez!" Spencer said, running after her.

They passed through three more tunnels—one made of soft cotton, one made of bouncy rubber, and one made of chocolate candy bars— and then stepped into the last tunnel before Weebleville, the fire tunnel. As Nikki marched between the torches hanging on each side of the tunnel, she licked chocolate off of her fingers. Spencer did the same. Anytime they passed through the chocolate bar tunnel they always ran their fingers along the walls to get them nice and chocolaty. "Mmm," they said together.

After a few minutes, the end of the tunnel came into view, a big stone door blocking their way. WEEBLEVILLE was written in shaky handwriting above the door. Loud voices were rumbling behind the stone, but Nikki couldn't understand what they were saying until she got closer.

Her eyes widened when she figured it out. The voices were chanting as one. "Power Island! Power Island! Power Island!"

Nikki and Spencer looked at each other, smiles forming on their lips. Together, they each grabbed a part of the door and heaved it open.

2

I am the greatest power kid

Naomi was tired of being angry all the time, but she couldn't seem to be happy anymore. She'd lost her biggest fight yet, all because of that annoying George Powerglasses guy. She'd also lost her entire gang of Power Outlaws when they joined Nikki's stupid Power Team.

"Stupid George," she muttered under her breath. "Stupid Power Team, stupid Power Giver." She looked at the skirt she was wearing, black with green polka dots. It gave her the ability to change her powers rapidly. Not that it mattered. It was pointless having powers when she wasn't even a part of the Power Rankings anymore. She was just an outcast now. "Stupid skirts."

Her sidekick, Slobber, wasn't really helping her mood. A few days ago he'd found a bucket of colored chalk. He'd been drawing pictures of the Power Team ever since. There was Nikki Powergloves and Freddy Powersocks and all the rest. He was even drawing their freaky little sidekicks. In fact, Slobber had just about finished his picture of the amateur magician, Chilly Weathers.

"Stupid sidekick," Naomi muttered.

"What wash that, bossh?" Slobber asked.

"Did I say you could speak?" Naomi said sharply, putting her hands on her hips.

"No, but—" A line of drool ran from Slobber's mouth to his drawings on the cement.

"Did I say you could drool?" Naomi asked.

"No, but—"

"Did I say you could do *anything?*"

Slobber closed his mouth, although spit continued to run down his chin.

"That's better," Naomi said. "You're MY sidekick. You jump when I say you can jump, you draw when I say you can draw, and you drool when I say you can drool."

Slobber drooled.

"Stop that!"

Using his shirt, Slobber wiped away the drool and clamped his lips together tightly, trying to hold back the spittle. Naomi looked her sidekick up and down. His shoes were untied and his shorts and shirt coated with powdery chalk dust. "Hmm," Naomi said. Unlike her, he was far from perfect. From a young age, Naomi's parent's had expected perfection from her. Getting the top score on a test was only good enough if she got 100%. Missing a single answer meant she'd have to study twice as hard for the next test. Once, when she got second place in a school spelling bee, her father was so angry that he made her walk home. "Win next time," he said. "Or you can walk everywhere." She won the next spelling bee, and the one after that, and every single competition since. Whatever it took, she had to win at everything she did, or she would disappoint her parents. And that included winning the Power Rankings.

Slobber's face was turning red. Naomi realized he was holding his breath. "Breathe!" she yelled. "You don't need my permission to breathe, stupid!"

Slobber released his breath and sucked in more air, slobbering all over his own shoes in the process. Naomi shook her head. If her sidekick wasn't so freakishly big and strong, he'd be completely useless. Instead, he was all she had left.

"Why do you keep drawing the Power Team?" she asked.

He looked startled, his hands clutching each other nervously. "I, um, I just, well—"

Naomi tapped her toe. "I don't have all day!" She didn't know why she kept shouting, but she couldn't seem to stop. She was just so...so...*angry*.

Slobber wiped away more drool and said, "I just thought maybe we could eventually, you know, join the Power Team."

"No," Naomi said immediately.

"But they've invited us."

Naomi didn't need to be reminded. Twice in the last two days that pathetic George Poweglasses dude had slid down his rainbow and handed her a card. Then he'd created a beautiful white Pegasus and flown away without saying a word. Naomi didn't have the cards anymore, because she'd ripped them into a thousand pieces and fed them to her flock of attack pigeons. Each card had said the same thing:

Naomi Powerskirts and sidekick Slobber,
   You are hereby invited to join the Power Team at your earliest convenience.
   Please don't wait too long or we'll be forced to leave for the Power Island without you.
   Meet us at Weebleville.
   Sincerely,
   George Powerglasses (on behalf of the Power Team)

Just thinking about their stupid message made Naomi cringe. Join them? Really? They were all a bunch of idiots who didn't know a great power from a freckle. But still...maybe her slobbering sidekick was on to something.

"You really want to join the Power Team, huh?" she asked.

Slobber nodded, drool spilling from his lips like a leaky faucet.

Naomi tapped her toe and cracked her knuckles, remembering how quickly Sue the Perfect Barbie Doll had joined the Power Team. Maybe Sue was just being sneaky. Maybe she was being smarter than Naomi. "Hmm," Naomi said. "Maybe you're right."

"I am?" Slobber said.

"Well, you said something smart, but I don't think you said it on purpose, so it's really *my* idea and not yours. Do you understand?"

Slobber just stared at her like a hideous reflection in the mirror. The anger rushed into Naomi like a crashing wave. Rapidly, she changed her skirt to her pink gymnastics one, did a double front flip with a twist, and landed on Slobber, knocking him hard to the ground. She stared down at him. "I said: Do. You. Understand?"

Eyes wider than traffic lights, he nodded.

"Good," Naomi said. "We'll leave immediately. We'll be joining the Power Team after all. But only so we can win. Only so we can destroy them all on the Power Island. Only so we can find the Power Giver and rise to the top of the Power Rankings."

"That doesn't sound very nice," Slobber said.

"I am the greatest power kid," Naomi said. "But not because I'm nice. Because I always win."

3

Butt-bouncin' good

"Power Island! Power Island! Power Island!" The chant got louder and louder as Nikki and Spencer walked through Weebleville. The streets were empty of both Weebles and kids, which was very unusual. Normally the Weebles would be dancing and playing. Instead, they'd left behind all their toys, inflatable beach balls and water guns and Nerf Frisbees and even rolls of white toilet paper.

"Power Island! Power Island! POWER ISLAND! POWER ISLAND!" As they got closer, the sound became deafening.

Nikki and Spencer dodged the debris, making their way to a big square in front of the tall tower where the Great Weeble lived. That's where they discovered the source of the noise.

"POWER ISLAND! POWER ISLAND!" chanted the Weebles and kids.

"Hey, Nikki! Spencer!" someone shouted. Nikki spotted Samantha in the crowd, pushing and shoving her way past the prickly porcupine-beavers to get to her.

"Hey, Sam," Nikki said. "Are we on time?"

Samantha smiled. "Yes, we're still waiting on a couple of power kids." It was hard to hear her friend's voice over the sound of the Weebles' chanting.

Amidst the cacophony, other members of the Power Team were crowding around them now too, Freddy and Mike and Britney and Tanya. Their sidekicks, Chilly and Dexter, were also there. Tyrone and his sidekick, Weasel, stood nearby. Weasel was balanced on Tyrone's shoulders and smirking at Nikki. Peter Powerhats was sitting behind the wheel of a giant monster truck, revving the engine. Sue and her sidekick, Sharkey, were pretending not to notice Nikki's arrival, but Nikki could tell they were watching very carefully. Even though Sue had joined the Power Team, Nikki still didn't really trust her. All she seemed to care about was herself and winning whatever prize the Power Giver was planning to give the winner of the Power Rankings.

Nikki considered who was still missing. "Where are Jimmy and Axel?" she asked.

Samantha shrugged. "No-shows so far."

Nikki really hoped Jimmy would come, but she knew he was still struggling with whether it was okay to use his powers. He had really changed since the first time she met him, when all he wanted to do was destroy things. Now he seemed to only want to help. "Tanya," Nikki said. "You've been talking to Jimmy a lot, right?"

Tanya ducked her head a little, as if surprised Nikki had asked her a question. "Well, yeah, I guess so." Her face was turning fire-engine red at all the attention.

"Do you think he'll come?" Nikki asked, smiling and nodding. Tanya sometimes needed to be encouraged to speak.

Tanya managed a small smile of her own and lifted her chin. "Yes. Yes, I think he'll come."

"Good. What about Axel?" Nikki asked. "Has anyone spoken to him and Juniper?"

Everyone shook their heads. Nikki's heart sank. Without Axel and his awesome sidekick, June the Goon, facing the Power Island would be far more difficult.

"They'll come too," Spencer said, patting her on the back. "I know it." Spencer's confidence made Nikki feel a little better. Her sidekick's predictions were almost always right.

"What about Naomi?" Tyrone asked, his strong voice carrying above the ruckus.

"What about her?" Sue said, finally coming closer.

"George said he invited her too," Tyrone said. "He said we'd have a better chance on the Power Island if Naomi joined the Power Team."

"Blech," Sue said. "We don't need her. Trust me, I know Naomi, and she's like a thorn stuck in your thumb that you can never get out."

For once, Nikki agreed with Sue. Naomi had never done anything but try to hurt her and her friends. Nikki really hoped Naomi stayed away from Weebleville until they were long gone and headed for the Power Island.

That's when Jimmy showed up. Well, more like walked right through one of the walls of the Great Weeble's tower. He was like a ghost, walking through the crowd, stepping right through the Weebles instead of going around them. Some of them giggled and bobbed up and down on their rear ends. "Jimmy's butt-bouncin' good!" one of them said.

Nikki didn't know what that meant, but seeing Jimmy made her smile. "Glad you could make it," she said, extending her hand for a high five.

Jimmy looked at her hand for a moment, chewing his lip, and then slapped it. "Thank you," he said. "I hope I can help the team."

"You will," Nikki said. "I know it."

Before Jimmy could respond, George Powerglasses appeared overhead, riding his snow-white Pegasus. As he soared over them, a cheer went up from the Weebles and kids, and then slowly died down, until there was complete silence. The Pegasus landed in the middle of the square, folding its purple wings at its sides. George's Google Glasses matched his flying horse's wings perfectly. Everyone waited for him to speak. Everyone except Sue.

"Is it *finally* time to go?" Sue asked. "Waiting to go to the Power Island is more boring than watching Spencer sort through his superhero underwear collection."

Nikki glared at Sue. She didn't care if Sue made fun of her, but it was not okay to make fun of her sidekick. The only problem was that

Spencer *did* like to sort through his superhero underwear collection and it *was* really boring.

Sue ignored Nikki and stared at George, waiting for his response.

George tipped his purple glasses down on his nose and looked out over the crowd. "I don't see Axel," he said.

"Who cares," Sue said. "We don't need him."

"Yes, we do," Nikki said, stepping forward.

"No, we don't," Sue said, moving closer to Nikki. Nikki had the urge to use her super-speed to run up to Sue and tackle her. She took a deep breath. *No,* she told herself. *We're supposed to be a team.*

Nikki didn't know what else to say, but thankfully George did. "Nikki's right," George said. "Without Axel, we're not leaving."

"Grrr," Sue growled in frustration. "I can't take another minute in this…this…*place*! These *creatures* are disgusting! Look at them!" All around Sue, the Weebles were bouncing on their butts, grinning big, toothy grins.

Nikki knew Naomi meant the Weebles, but she didn't think of them as creatures, and they certainly weren't disgusting. Mildly rude and sometimes irritating, yeah, but mostly funny and weird. She considered the Weebles to be her friends.

Luckily, Axel showed up just when it looked like Sue might start using the Weebles as kick balls. He was in slinky form, rattling toward them in long slinky strides. Dark-haired Juniper was riding Axel the Slinky, leaping from prong to prong with each step. She looked awesome.

"Finally!" Sue said.

Axel transformed back into himself. He was wearing a heavy gray wool jacket with a picture of a slinky on it. He was also wearing a mischievous grin as he looked at his watch. "Right on time," he said in a strong English accent.

"Sorry," June said, apologizing for her superhero. "He insisted on waiting until the last possible minute. I've been trying to get him to come for hours."

Nikki didn't care about any of that. She was just glad Axel was here. Now the entire Power Team was in one place at one time. Surely that meant they could leave for the Power Island.

"You're still missing one power kid," George said.

Nikki frowned. "What? No, everyone's here." She looked around, trying to see if she'd forgotten anyone. *Nope.*

"Naomi," George said.

"But you said we could go without her," Sue complained.

"I lied," George said. "The Power Giver won't let any of you on the Power Island unless *all* of you go. You have to be a team."

Sue blew out an exasperated breath. "This is a waste of time. Naomi will never show." Sharkey clacked her teeth together in agreement.

"She might," George said.

Sue balled her fists and looked ready to face George *and* his Pegasus. "If you think Naomi is going to show her face around here, you're even dumber than you loo—"

There was a flash of light and Naomi appeared, with Slobber standing at her side, blinking away spots from his eyes.

"Hey losers," Naomi said, winking right at Nikki. "Did you miss me?"

Nikki Powergloves and the Power Giver is available NOW!

28430961R00093

Made in the USA
Middletown, DE
14 January 2016